The Intriguing Cases of

BLACKTHORN PANTHER, PI

England's Unlikely Yet Lovable Detective

JONTY OLIVIER

**The Panther Chronicles
Book One**

An Eagle Eye Publication

Eagle Eye Consultancy UK, Ltd
Jontyolivier.com

Publisher's Note: This is a work of fiction. Names, characters, places, and incidents are a product of the author's imagination. Locales and public names are sometimes used to create a certain atmosphere. Any resemblance to actual people, living or dead, or to businesses, companies, events, institutions, or locales is completely coincidental.

The Intriguing Cases of Blackthorn Panther, PI / Jonty Olivier
— 1st ed.
ISBN 978-0-9996283-2-4 paperback
ISBN 978-0-9996283-3-1 ebook
Library of Congress Control Number: 2018943007

For Janie with love

In kind recognition of George P. and Peter M.

ACKNOWLEDGEMENTS

First, abundant thanks to my book midwife, Ruth Schwartz, who continues to impress me in everything she does. Without her, this book would most likely remain solely on my desktop. Huge thanks to Janie Tongue for her unwavering support including the initial draft of the front cover which was expertly crafted into reality by Christine Holmes of White Rabbit Graphix. Additional special thanks to Becky Parker Geist at ProAudioVoices for insightful comments and suggestions that undoubtedly helped improve the final product. Finally, to George P. and Peter M. who took on a young ex-police officer in 1978 when expanding their detective and security business. Without their total trust and implicit faith in that young man's abilities, none of the content from these pages would have been possible.

AUTHOR'S NOTE

DOES IT TAKE AN AMATEUR SLEUTH to enjoy a detective story? Not at all, obviously, yet it might help provide a little background. A number of the physical places in this book actually exist but names have been changed. Whilst content should be treated as fictional, many details are based on similar real-life personal experiences. I truly did leave the police and become a private investigator under circumstances close to those endured by Blackthorn, and the hit-and-run motorcycle accident depicted in Chapter Four did happen.

My first meeting with the George McPullis character is invented, although a real George influenced me greatly and was a private detective of international standing. I considered him a mentor and friend who is greatly missed by those who knew him. I owe much to George and his business partner, Peter, both of whom trusted me despite a lack of experience to successfully complete an array of tricky cases. I reveled in the responsibilities thrust upon me and enjoyed just about every minute of each, even the dangerous ones.

The stories take place in England and generally British English has been used throughout. For my non-British readers, I trust that you will manage to learn a few English words and phrases as you delve through Blackthorn's adventures.

This book is the first of a series of four, each containing four of my most memorable cases. Again, a reminder that this is a work of fiction though much is indeed inspired by real events. However, I absolutely did attend a nightclub dressed as a wolf and my buddy as a vicar, as described, on the wrong event night (Chapter Eight). Did I meet Charli in that lupine attire or did she even exist at all? That must, for now at least, remain a closely regarded secret—all will be revealed in the fourth book in the series.

Chapter One

THE SPEEDOMETER HITS EIGHTY-FIVE and the streets are a blur! This is the first time Blackthorn has been at the wheel of a Jaguar and it's fast, too fast maybe, but he's playing catch-up. The bank robbers have a head start and there's no police in sight. It's down to him and him alone to chase and catch the bad guys. Engines scream. Tyres screech and smoke. Those baddies are crazy and still a few hundred yards ahead. They slice their way through the sedate afternoon traffic. They're sure to kill someone at this rate. Sleepy Swinborough has never seen such a thing.

Pedestrians scatter for their lives at a bus stop as the getaway car skids around a corner, narrowly missing them, and a cyclist is forced to dive through a shop window to escape certain death. Motorists veer off the road in a desperate need for self-preservation.

Blackthorn is at last, catching those rogues as they slow for red traffic lights ahead. Those simply out on a shopping trip or on their way to a meeting innocently block the road ahead, patiently waiting for the lights to change. The villains have other ideas though, as they once more accelerate and carve their way between two lanes of vehicles, battering them violently out of the way. The Jaguar follows through the created opening and Blackthorn is determined more than ever to save the day.

Right must overcome evil.

A humpbacked bridge lies ahead but there are no brake lights from the lead car as it soars into the air and momentarily disappears out of view. Blackthorn releases the right pedal and brakes hard, forcing him into a semi-standing position off his seat. A woman pushing a pram appears from nowhere, crossing the bridge directly in harm's way. Still braking, Blackthorn spins the steering wheel sharply to the left. The Jaguar skids violently and mounts the curb, crashing head-on into the low wall of the brick bridge where it comes to an abrupt stop, hanging precariously above the river below.

A huge explosion grabs his attention and he catches sight of the bad guys' car bursting into flames as it collides with a fuel tanker. While black-topped flames and thick, dark smoke plumes into the Swinborough sky, Blackthorn feels the Jaguar rock slightly and its nose begin to dip. He pushes against the partially open driver's door. Piles of bricks prevent it from moving further. He's trapped, and now he can smell fuel.

His gaze through the shattered windscreen is interrupted by a stream of warm blood from a head wound. He feels for it, hoping to stem the flow but just moments later, as if triggered by a second blast from the tanker crash further down the road, the Jaguar inches further forward. There's no stopping it now with momentum taking over. As it plummets from its precarious position, he crosses his heart, squeezes his eyes tightly shut and waits for the inevitable impact with the water below.

Chapter Two

HE AWAKENS WITH A START. He's sweating but alive. He looks around. No river. No Jaguar and no bridge. His fingers seek out a non-existent wound. The lack of blood tells its own story. He must get more sleep. He gently slaps both sides of his face and stretches his eyes as wide as they'll go. Drifting off on a surveillance case is simply not on. He chastises himself before briefly noting that there's been zero change to what's going on outside. He returns to his scribbles of earlier on.

Blackthorn Panther is the greatest private investigator of 1980 and probably of all time. Blackthorn Panther solves the most complex of cases. Blackthorn Panther is the new Sherlock Holmes or Hercule Poirot.

Twenty-four-year-old Blackthorn Panther continues to pen such aspirations into his tiny notebook. He's excited and hoping for a high-speed car chase in this latest case, worthy of comparison to the one out of the Mad Max movie that he saw a few months back. There's no doubt that the movie has left an indelible imprint on his expectations around pursuing villains. He's primed and ready to blaze a trail wherever the action takes him. He's now even dreaming about it!

Truth is, when awake at least, he's been fidgeting in his car seat for almost two hours, parked up in a muddy grass field entrance on a lonely lane in rural Woldshire. His clunker of a rental car from Beat Ups Beat Down Car Hire Swinborough Limited isn't up to much either. It has seen better days for sure. The cloth seats are faded, the dashboard sports a strange, mottled look as though acid has been poured across it, and the radio doesn't work. There are several dents and numerous scratches to its bodywork, none of which are listed on the hire document that lays neatly folded on the passenger seat. He had needed a car that was cheap but reliable and this Volvo seemed ideal. Powerful enough to keep up in a high-speed pursuit but ordinary enough not to arouse suspicion, and that was his main concern here. It is a blend-in sort of car, anonymous and nondescript, a bit like Blackthorn himself. Five feet ten inches, medium build, okay-looking, he reckons. The quintessential Mister Average. He and this Volvo make a great surveillance team.

Parked up on a lane of high hedgerows and even taller trees, he had backed into this field entrance with the rear bumper almost touching a crooked gate. Set back from the road and well-hidden, he was perfectly positioned to keep an eye on Dastardly Donald. He likes to give his subjects nicknames to keep his cases more interesting during the occasional dull times, and to aid memory.

Donald Jones has been accused by his wife, Patricia, of having an affair, which of course, he's denied. She is convinced though, and after several severe anxiety attacks allegedly brought about by her husband's possible infidelity, she has, at last, decided to do something about it.

Thumbing through The Yellow Pages, Poor Patricia had called the only listed Private Investigation Agency, Deutschland Detectives, but they had been much too busy right now to help and had suggested she call back in a couple of weeks. Blackthorn is aware of them, of course. It's run by two German brothers—Hugo and Otto Schneider—and according to a few of Blackthorn's clients, are often too busy to help, which on a positive front, seems to suggest that there is plenty of work to go around for both firms.

Luckily for Blackthorn, a concerned girlfriend of Poor Patricia had recommended she call a number she'd come across in the classified ads of the local paper. That is where Blackthorn Panther goes fishing for work. Much cheaper than proper advertising—and it works. The ad is sheer genius in Blackthorn's eyes. It goes like this:

SHERLOCK HOLMES or HERCULE POIROT. This Is Now Where You Must Go. Private Investigations Are My Thing. So Don't Delay, Get Up and Ring. Swinborough 299492.

He normally receives two or three calls a week and all are fielded by his latest toy, a very cool answer-machine that goes by the name of Ellen and doubles as his personal assistant. She sits dutifully alongside a two-tone Trimphone dedicated to The Queen's Silver Jubilee of three years earlier, a house-warming gift from his mum. He hopes in the future to have a real live P.A. but Ellen is the best he can afford right now. Her outgoing message goes like this:

"Thank you for calling Panther Investigations. Just like real panthers, we're experts at camouflage, have excellent day and night vision, climb trees and when we get our prey, we tear it apart with our sharp claws. Just joking that last part but it's a jungle out there and I'm here to get great results for you. Leave a message and I'll be seeing you soon."

Blackthorn thinks that one day, he might like to write newspapers ads or even television commercials, but for now, he's proud to be a Private Investigator and happy enough.

He checks the notes he took during his meeting with Poor Patricia. As he doesn't have an office and his tiny fourth floor apartment is hardly business-like, he usually conducts his interviews—as he likes to call them—in local pubs. He recalls seeing Patricia Jones for the first time. Mid to late thirties probably, slim, mousy hair and although quite nice looking and almost pretty, was sad. So sad. It was the sad eyes that did it for him.

"Poor Patricia," he had whispered to himself as she approached, and the name stuck.

His notes are tiny scribbles perfectly sized for his tiny notebook. They're illegible to anyone except himself and like a secret code that even his clients, should they inadvertently get a glimpse, would never be able to decipher. They read that Dastardly Donald has recently begun leaving home around seven o'clock some evenings to go meet work colleagues but evades giving names, a location or a firm time to return. He has never done this before. It's so out of character. If that doesn't arouse suspicion, what does? The client instructions are clear.

Follow him and find out what he's up to and who he's meeting. Then report back.

Importantly, he's told Poor Patricia that he's going out again tonight. The problem for Blackthorn is that it's already well past eight o'clock and Dastardly Donald still appears to be at home. From his vantage point, Blackthorn can see the subject's house one hundred yards away. He takes a photograph with his new Nikon F3 SLR given by his mum as an early birthday present. He loves his mum, not just because she supports his dreams with useful gadgets, but for her show of unwavering faith in him when it would be so easy to criticize his recent career choices.

A loose-stoned drive entrance is a short distance from where he now sits. The hedge opposite, though sparse, offers valuable cover while allowing for a perfectly good view of the house under observation. It's a modest detached period property that reminds him of a parsonage he once knew as a child. Lights inside are on and there are two cars on the gravel drive. The tiny notes are clear—to Blackthorn and only Blackthorn. Dastardly Donald's car is a black Ford Capri and Poor Patricia's a white Ford Fiesta. He smirks. Is everything in this case to be so black and white and why hasn't Dastardly Donald gone out yet?

Blackthorn doodles on a page of his tiny notebook. The evening shadows are now long, and it will be dark soon. He has accepted a holding deposit from Poor Patricia of twenty-five pounds for this case and decides he is going to give her his best shot. He'll wait just another half an hour before reluctantly abandoning tonight's efforts. There's bound to be another night. These things happen. Par for the course, confides a voice in his head.

Only a handful of vehicles pass his hiding place in the lane during his time here. It really is in the sticks. He gets out of the car to stretch his legs. It is quiet, almost too quiet. No traffic noise, not even a bird singing for its supper. The contrails of an aircraft passing silently high overhead remind him that he's not the only one still alive on the planet. It's a warm mid-August evening and the familiar rays of the on-coming sunset light up the western sky. The sipping of a couple of cans of Vimto over the past couple of hours has eventually taken its toll and he feels the urge to pee.

The hedge ditch alongside makes a perfectly concealed outlet. Relief is welcome but timing not great. Approaching full stream, he hears a car crunching over the stones of the nearby driveway and looks across at the house. In the late evening gloom, he strains to see detail but manages to detect an empty car space. The Capri is gone! He finishes as quickly as nature will allow, splashes his shoes and jumps back into the Volvo. He starts it up with a roar—or with as much of a roar that the Volvo can muster. With a back-end slide to the left and mud splattering the gate, the car skids out into the lane, spilling remnants of a Vimto can as it drops to the floor, just in time to see car lights shining on the tree-lined hill further up the lane speeding away from him. A pursuit is on and the soundtrack to Mad Max bursts into his head!

Chapter Three

FOLLOWING ANYONE BY CAR IN A TOWN OR CITY can be tricky due to traffic lights, pedestrians and other motorists getting in the way, but concealment is relatively easy. When in pursuit of the only other vehicle on the road, that becomes a tad more difficult. Blackthorn puts the old Volvo through its paces as he plays catch up with the Capri. Dastardly Donald sure drives fast and Blackthorn prays that there's no meeting of oncoming traffic in the narrow lane. Speedometer indicates fifty-five m.p.h. but it feels much faster on such a dicey strip of rough road. The lane veers left and right, rises and falls and it's that time of day when some drivers use their car lights, and some do not. It's a dangerous time to drive down a lane that is tricky at the best of times. Blackthorn negotiates a particularly sharp bend and instantly, is forced to slam on his brakes.

Mr. Volvo is built like a tank and catches the loose gravel on the road surface. Blackthorn's heart is in his mouth as he slides towards the back of the Capri that has only minimal forward momentum and displays no brake lights. But it does have two Volvo headlights blazing into its rear window and they're getting closer by the milli-second. With just a few inches remaining and Blackthorn's eyes squeezed tight, Mr. Volvo decides to come to a nose-dipping and grinding halt.

"Phew! Crash averted," he gasps. Forthcoming altercation, not quite so much.

Blackthorn slumps back into his seat. The Capri inches forward several feet and then displays brake lights. They're shortly replaced by hazard warning lights. The driver's door is flung open, and he who presumably is Dastardly Donald steps out and glares back at Blackthorn. He does not look a happy-chappy. Blackthorn is not easily intimidated but for reasons best known to himself, chooses at that moment to stay inside his car. He doesn't make a single movement.

Dastardly Donald is ranting and throwing his arms around as would an energetic mime artist.

Something about driving like a—it's a little difficult hearing exactly what is being said but the gist is perfectly clear. He is not overrating Blackthorn's driving speed on such a road and is apparently, lucky to be alive. Blackthorn sighs. No drama there then and what about my brilliant braking abilities? Don't I get credit for anything?

Dastardly Donald strides purposefully halfway towards the Volvo, then thankfully, stops. He has another ten second rant, waves his right arm in a dismissive sort of way in Blackthorn's direction, and then sprints the short distance back to the Capri, presumably remembering the urgency of his evening jaunt into the arms of another—allegedly of course. Blackthorn notices that his new adversary is a taller version of Poor Patricia, skinny like her and obviously a bit highly strung. He is dressed casually and not overly out to impress. Blackthorn concludes that outwardly at least, the couple appear ideal for each other. Shame really, he concludes. What a pity Dastardly Donald seems to have his brains in his trousers.

The Capri creeps forward with its hazard warning lights now extinguished. Brake lights are on though as it crawls along at less than walking pace. Then Blackthorn sees them. A brace of ducks waddling down the lane. The Capri inches past them and then quickly speeds off, but not before Dastardly Donald makes a less than complimentary hand gesture in his rearview mirror. The Capri lights disappear around another corner as Mr. Volvo also slowly and respectfully passes the ducks. Blackthorn winds down the side window. "Thanks, Ducks," he calls sarcastically.

They ignore him, their collective waddle never missing a beat.

But then he feels bad. Those ducks will surely die if nothing is done to save them. The next car around that corner is sure to register a kill. He instantly formulates a plan. He drives forward about thirty yards, then stops and engages reverse gear. There's nowhere wide enough to turn around and thankfully, no other traffic. He backs up at speed with the car horn blasting, then comes to a screeching halt. He's beginning to get good at this severe braking lark. Low and behold, and to his amazement, it does the trick. Whilst obviously impervious to fast cars going forward, the ducks scatter, scrambling up the steeply-sided bank, into and through the high hedge above. One takes flight and disappears over the hedge to meet its mates. Blackthorn feels good about himself, but only for a moment or two.

Dastardly Donald has got away.

Blackthorn decides that there is absolutely no way he is likely to catch up with Dastardly Donald and proceeds onward at a slow, safe speed that his grandfather would be proud of. He is wondering what explanation he is going to give to Poor Patricia, though he does have a valid excuse. Dastardly Donald had left home much later than anticipated. Many PI's would have already left and gone home and missed the car chase opportunity altogether. It was only down to his superior professionalism and due diligence that he noticed the Capri at all, he speculates.

He approaches a T-junction where the lane meets the main road and there is no sign of the Capri. Left goes to the nearby town of Marlsham; right goes way out into the country.

Where would someone go who is having an illicit affair? Out into a little country pub or restaurant perhaps, or to her house. They may even have located a field gate somewhere, he smiles.

Then there's the town option. Lots of people and easy to blend in but more chance of being seen by someone they know. He begins to turn right, then suddenly and violently swerves left at the last second and, on an infamous Blackthorn Panther hunch, heads for Marlsham.

It takes just twenty minutes for Blackthorn to reach the small town and he begins his search in its centre, the historic marketplace. He crawls slowly past several pubs and hotels, driving in and out of car parks and spots several Ford Capris, two of them black. He checks out the plates and bingo! What a stroke of luck! The second one is the one! It has taken less than five minutes to track down Dastardly Donald. He has parked outside The Olde Waggon & Horses Inn and Blackthorn is quickly inside.

The inn is surprisingly busy for a Tuesday. Maybe trivial quiz night? There are two bars, both with gnarled black wood seating throughout plus several smaller lounge rooms. Ceilings are low and heavy timbers adorn both ceilings and walls. A heady cocktail of beer and ancient wood—or should that be ancient beer and wood—lays heavily in the air. He checks out both main bars but it's not until he enters one of the smaller rooms that he notices Dastardly Donald, and as suspected, he is not alone.

Dastardly Donald is snuggled away, almost from view, in a far calculated corner, sipping a half pint of beer or similar and his lady companion is seated alongside, too close for comfort some might say— Poor Patricia would most definitely say. The empty bottle on the table indicates she's drinking tonic water. It's not possible for Blackthorn to deduce whether it has an alcoholic additive or not. He returns to the main bar and orders a tomato juice with Worcestershire Sauce and ice. Not shaken but stirred quite a lot.

He retraces his steps and sits at a pew-like seat which gives him the view he needs. The couple he has in his proverbial crosshairs are friendly with each other—very friendly. They have a touchy-feely relationship, and obviously like each other a lot. They take it in turns to write things down in a large notebook on the bench table before them. Ah, a large notebook. What it would be like to have a large notebook? Blackthorn jokes to himself. So, what are they planning? Their next escape somewhere? A trip to some exotic resort? Ideas on how to break the news to Poor Patricia? How to do away with Poor Patricia?

So many thoughts almost overwhelm Blackthorn but as he contemplates their devilish activity, he is also mildly surprised that Dastardly Donald and his new woman do not even hold hands. He observes that their legs and feet do not entwine or engage with each other, nor does the couple kiss, or come close to doing so.

They're just playing clever, being careful as they chose the town option, he logically suggests. Blackthorn estimates that the woman is roughly the same age as Poor Patricia. She is similar in stature to Poor Patricia too but has lots of tumbling blonde locks. Do blondes really have more fun? Was it her hair that first attracted Dastardly Donald? He very carefully frees the Nikon from under his light summer jacket and fakes a cough. A few seconds later, another cough provides cover as another photo is added.

Blackthorn is confident that Dastardly Donald does not recognize him from their earlier altercation. The distance between them during that unfortunate incident had been considerable for the untrained eye, he believes.

The fact of the matter is that Dastardly Donald has much more pressing stuff on his mind right now. The issue in the lane is probably long forgotten as he beams the evening away with the mystery lady at The

Olde Waggon and Horses Inn. They chat, laugh and plot their way through precisely another fifty-seven minutes before standing. They hug briefly and walk out. She carries the large notebook tucked safely under her arm and he follows a discreet distance behind.

They're good at this. Very good, notes Blackthorn. As they leave the inn, the couple turn to each other, hug again and Dastardly Donald kisses his new friend on each cheek. Very French, thinks Blackthorn, as he records every embrace with the Nikon. He watches from the inn entrance as the couple go their separate ways. She gets into a blue Mercedes saloon and he into his Capri. The Mercedes is also captured on film with all its identifying details. They set off in opposite directions.

Ever the professional, Blackthorn follows Dastardly Donald within moderate and then light traffic to the T-junction with the lane and sees him head for home. Never one to presume, he waits two minutes before entering the lane, slowly making his way, wary of an onset of suicidal ducks, back to the home currently shared by Poor Patricia and Dastardly Donald, but for how much longer? As he passes the end of their drive, he notices the Capri parked on the drive next to the Fiesta. It had been a long evening and it was time to head home.

Wednesday morning is busy for Blackthorn. He locates his typewriter and his Panther Investigations letterhead paper from a kitchen cupboard. The paper displays a black paw print logo with a strap line underneath: *Panther Tracks for You*. He completes his report.

Early that afternoon, around one o'clock, the phone rings. He's ready. The report is complete in a large manila envelope accompanied with several photos, none of which are particularly incriminating but hopefully useful to his client. Poor Patricia is on the end of the line as agreed. She asks how he got on. Blackthorn delivers a brief overview and arranges to meet her later that week to hand over the report in full, together with photographs and to collect the balance payment of a further twenty pounds plus expenses of twenty-six pounds and thirty-two pence.

It's Friday and Blackthorn and Poor Patricia meet outside in the car-park of The Old Town Hotel in south Swinborough. She hands over the cash and he the envelope containing the report and photos developed by his friend Pete. She is hesitant, almost reluctant, and close to tears.

"It's best to know these things," states Blackthorn with an air of wisdom beyond his years. She accepts with trembling fingers.

"I'll look at everything later," she says tearfully and leaves. He feels sorry for her all over again. Poor Patricia.

Blackthorn runs some errands, goes shopping and returns home. The moment he opens the door, Ellen is again busy. He immediately recognizes the voice on the machine. Poor Patricia is crying. No! More than that. Much more than that. She's hysterical! She's screaming, calling someone a lying bitch and much more besides.

Blackthorn picks up and forcefully attempts to interrupt, but it takes a while. She is one angry lady. He discovers that the mystery woman who met her husband is her best friend. They have been best friends since they were teenagers at school. "How could they?" she weeps.

Blackthorn does his best to offer platitudes and is quick to point out that in his considered opinion, the investigation was in its infancy and that much more was required to prove that anything was going on, as he politely puts it.

Minutes pass and she is now calm, or at least a percentage or two calmer than she was. "No more talk. No more investigating, Mr. Panther. It's time to confront." She thanks Blackthorn for his help and hangs up. There'll be trouble in the hills tonight, he wagers.

On Saturday, Blackthorn has a rare day off. He finds himself between cases and spends some quality down time with a couple of friends. They visit a few bars before hitting a Chinese takeaway late that evening and he returns home alone around ten thirty. Ellen is flashing for him and he turns her on. It's Poor Patricia, but she's not hysterical this time. She is speaking quietly and slowly.

"Oh, my goodness. I am so sorry Mr. Panther. I hardly know where to start. Look, I've made a terrible mistake. I want to let you know that my darling husband has been planning with my best friend for my upcoming fortieth birthday party next week. They've assured me that it was to be a huge surprise and have even shown me some of the plans they've made. Not all obviously because they want to keep some ideas up their sleeves. Anyway, the upshot is that all is well and thank you again. I won't be needing your services any longer. Thanks for everything." As what appears to be an afterthought, she adds in a more resolute tone, "I just want to say that I have a wonderful loving husband and the best, best friend in the whole wide world. Bye." And she hangs up.

So Dastardly Donald wasn't so dastardly after all. He was more like Dreamboat Donald, but Blackthorn will always remember him as Dastardly Donald Duck.

Even Poor Patricia isn't so poor anymore. Maybe she's managed, at last, to transform into Pretty Patricia.

And that was that. Another case closed. Another Chinese takeaway consumed and another week of exciting adventures to look forward to for Blackthorn Panther.

Chapter Four

BLACKTHORN HAD LEARNED JUST A FEW MONTHS earlier at the South & Midlands Private Investigators Convention held in Birmingham, that he was the youngest PI in the entire United Kingdom, not that it bothered him one bit. Sure, he got some looks from the seasoned pros and sensed on more than one occasion that those around him believed him to be out of his depth and not worthy to even be present in their distinguished company.

Not so George McPullis, who was as seasoned as they come, but still a nice, genuine guy who warmed to Blackthorn from the off. George seemed to celebrate the exuberance of youth in Blackthorn, citing more than once that not all PI's should be of retirement age which, Blackthorn observed, many were. George was intrigued why such a young man would choose to be a private investigator when so many other opportunities presumably lay before him.

Blackthorn had related his life story to George over a few beers at the conference hotel bar one evening and the Scot soon understood the young man's reasoning. He listened intently, fascinated at his story which went something like this.

Blackthorn had attended The Elizabethan Grammar School in Harteringham and been a popular pupil, doing well in those few academic subjects that interested him—and terrible in those that didn't. But generally, even those he preferred got in the way of his real love—sports, all sports. He was a tennis champion, a field hockey, football, badminton and cricket player who excelled in each, and loved every single second of the competition they offered.

He had enjoyed aspirations of becoming a professional sportsman, of achieving greatness on both national and international stages. He had left school with what he referred to as meaningless certificates and attended numerous trials with county teams in a variety of sports, all without the success he craved or expected. His prowess on the tennis court, however, promised more and he was shortly to travel to attend a national training camp. However, fate would play a part in altering his life.

At aged seventeen, he had taken out his fifth-hand Suzuki 80cc motorcycle that had cost him twenty-three pounds, for an early evening ride around the little town of Stourmead. The year was 1973 and it had become UK law earlier that year for motorcycle riders to wear a crash helmet when riding. The law had been passed despite much opposition and Blackthorn had been happy to conform. Commonsense dictated his stance. That day was to provide a pivotal turning point in his life.

He had been riding within a thirty-miles per hour speed limit on the outskirts of town. The street lights bathed the road in an orange glow and all appeared safe for the cautious learner-rider Blackthorn. Then suddenly, from a side road, a car had swerved out at high speed and struck the Suzuki with force. All Blackthorn recalls from the accident is an almighty thump and in the next instant, lying alongside the car with his head, complete with crash helmet, underneath it and just in front of a rear wheel.

There had been much commotion going on inside the car, a girl screaming loudly. He still recalls that to this very day. His body had felt awkward and twisted but without obvious pain. Almost by instinct, he had sensed the car was about to drive off. Whether it had been brought about by engine noise or something else, his intuition had probably saved his life. The car wheels moved forward and in that split second, he had somehow managed to summon all his strength and bend his neck to roll clear of the accelerating tyre by a mere fraction. He had looked across the road surface to see a Ford Cortina speed away, complete with a large dent in its side, no doubt. Under the orange lights, it had been impossible to discern the exact color of the car. It and the perpetrators within were never traced. Sadly, it was the end of the road for the Suzuki that lay buckled and twisted on an adjacent embankment, more than fifty feet away.

Blackthorn's injuries were never life-threatening but extremely inconvenient nevertheless. With dislocations to his left collar bone, left knee, left wrist and multiple abrasions, he had counted himself lucky. He recalls vividly the condition of the crash helmet. It was embedded with road stone and heavily scratched. If that had been direct head trauma, survival would have been unlikely. The result was he had been forced to miss the tennis camp and hadn't played since.

It had taken about ten weeks to fully recover from the crash injuries and following a long talk with his father, he had decided to join The Western Counties Police in which he had dutifully served until October of last year. Dad was a Military Police Officer and serving in uniform had its attraction to an impressionable—but determined to make a mark—young Blackthorn. He had no problem with the initial training and had done well in the years preceding his premature resignation.

"Such a shame for you," lamented George. "I was in the Mid-Scotland Force for many a year and enjoyed it immensely. What went wrong?"

Blackthorn further explained that he had become disillusioned with police life due to the poor pay and specifically, the attitude of some ambitious officers who appeared to care more about the length of his hair than how good he was at his job. One day, he decided out of the blue, to tender his resignation. It came as a shock to both his colleagues and the guilt-ridden pain-in-the-backside officers. The Assistant Chief Constable even attempted to dissuade him from his decision, but his mind was made up. He was certain that his parents, particularly his dad, would be disappointed—but to their credit, never once gave him a hard time about it. His mum had told him, "Just be happy, son, in whatever you choose to do." He could always rely on Mum.

His favourite time in the police had been spent with the Criminal Investigation Department. Surprisingly, he had loved being out of uniform, playing an active role investigating an array of cases which included fraud, burglary, arson, drug busts, theft, an undercover operation and even a murder. His parents at that time moved from near Swinborough to Tellingford, about a hundred miles to the north, due to his dad retiring because of ill health and wanting to return to his roots. Blackthorn preferred the Swinborough area and decided just before Christmas 1979, that he would open a private investigation agency there in the new year. He would be his own boss, make his own decisions, build a business, do what he loved to do and best of all, grow his hair as long as he damn well pleased. And he had done precisely that.

Chapter Five

ELLEN IS BUSY. BUSIER THAN NORMAL. There are three recorded messages waiting and it's only ten thirty on Monday morning. Blackthorn enjoyed a few too many beers last night at the Fox & Badger and though he can hear each ring, sometimes the body is weak and the mind unwilling. The phone sounds as though it's far away, in another apartment perhaps or on the far side of a hill. As Ellen kicks in and intercepts each call, he drifts back off, hearing just faint muffled voices. He'll get around to them soon enough.

He gulps down a pint of water and Ellen is soon put into action. The first message is from his mum. She urges him to look after himself, hope he has a lovely week and to please give her a call. She has a new recipe she wants him to try.

He gazes over to the sideboard where a photo of his parents takes pride of place inside a curled teak frame. He misses them so much since their move to Tellingford and he now gets to see them all too rarely. Mum is a retired nurse who spends her days cooking and cleaning. Dad has not been well for some time but manages to partake in a glass or two each day of Dry Blackthorn Cider, his preferred drink for many a year and the reason why young baby Panther is named as he is, or so the story goes. Just imagine had Dad's go-to drink been Hofmeister or God forbid, Babycham? The horrific possibilities are endless. Thank goodness for Blackthorn.

The sideboard is one of the few pieces of furniture that Blackthorn possesses. The apartment is sparsely furnished to say the least. There's an MFI TV cabinet housing a small TV and a mini-transistor radio in one corner. The cabinet had taken Blackthorn almost an entire day to assemble. DIY is not his strong point and when he triumphantly completed this most difficult of tasks, there remained two complete packets of screws left over. Had he owned a spirit level, he was sure the entire unit would be found leaning to the left. To complete the sitting room, there is a small drop leaf Formica table, with two matching chairs and a two-seater sofa, in a blue velvety fabric that he'd purchased at a second-hand store. The absence of any degree of interior design expertise is highlighted by the fact there isn't even a carpet. He intends to get one soon, of course, but there are more pressing matters right now, such as paying the rent on time.

Message number two reinforces this. He listens to the landlord kindly reminding him that the rent is due this week. He's receiving this gentle reminder because he's paid a few days late over the last couple of months. Ellen springs into action at the touch of a button and the reminder is deleted.

The number three glows in its red digital format. Ellen has something else to say.

"Good morning Panther. George here from Oxburton Detective Bureau. I have a case for you. Bloody gout and lumbago playing me up again, I'm afraid," he grumbles. "Can't get out of bed. Hope you can help. It's a good 'un and truth be known, it's on your patch, geographically speaking. Call me, young man, as soon as you can."

George conveys a mix of disappointment and excitement. Blackthorn is happy to hear from him. Despite the considerable disparity in age, they'd formed a close bond. George was very old school and following his time as a Police Detective north of the border, has been a PI for about fifteen years in Oxburton, only forty miles to the east of Swinborough. He had assured Blackthorn that he'd come across almost everything in his time serving Queen and Country, as he put it, and that had put him in good stead to be a successful PI. Sadly, he was not in the best of fettle nowadays, and had promised to pass on to Blackthorn any cases he was unable to start or complete himself due to his declining health. This was the first time since the convention that George had been in contact and it sounded promising. Blackthorn makes the call.

Chapter Six

G EORGE HAD BEEN RIGHT. This is proving to be Blackthorn's most lucrative case so far in a PI career spanning just six months. He is in familiar territory, the Woldshire sticks. He stops his Honda CB400 motorcycle that he calls Wanda alongside the sign for the hamlet of Little Belwain. Although it lies only twenty-two miles from his town apartment, it feels like a different world out here.

Blackthorn has received his initial deposit of two hundred and fifty pounds with a further two hundred and fifty pounds plus expenses to follow. A bonus of yet another two hundred and fifty will be paid upon a successful outcome. The two PI's have reached an agreement where George will receive twenty-five percent of the total payment for his referral.

The client is a renown London law firm that is attempting to enforce a court appearance by a gentleman who lives here in Little Belwain. His attendance is reported to be paramount to the outcome of an extremely important civil case, but this gentleman is reluctant to attend—so say the lawyers. Blackthorn's notes infer that this gentleman is genuinely ill, claiming to suffer from muscular dystrophy to such an extent that he is not only wheelchair-bound, but susceptible to a condition called cardiomyopathy which can lead to heart failure and death. Not good and he is point-blank refusing to travel to London to attend a court hearing that could be instrumental in his own demise.

Blackthorn Panther cannot help but feel sorry for this guy and has instantaneous empathy for his situation, but it is claimed that there is a rather large fly in this particular ointment. It is alleged that this gentleman has been put under pressure from certain third parties not to give evidence in these court proceedings and as recently as five weeks ago had willingly agreed to attend, only to cancel with less than twenty-four hours' notice of proceedings getting underway, citing a serious relapse in his health that prevented any travel plans.

Blackthorn had earlier studied the six-page letter of instructions supplied to him from the law firm that highlighted this being no less than the third time a last-minute cancellation had been received from this gentleman and something now had to be done. The crux of the entire problem appears to be that few at court believe that this guy is ill at all, seriously or otherwise.

A private doctor's report supplied by this gentleman outlining his illness is widely regarded as spurious, exaggerated or simple baloney. Attempts to gain access to him to obtain a second medical opinion have been rejected. A helicopter was even chartered to gain damning aerial evidence, but none was discovered.

In a new development in the case three weeks ago, his lawyer stated categorically that any attempt to subpoena his client to enforce his attendance will be fought most vehemently due to the distress this will likely cause. His client's subsequent probable death will be attributed to those electing such an inhumane course of action. They will have blood on their hands, it was succinctly put. This strong stance has proven sufficient to dissuade such an endeavour. It was therefore decided to adamantly disprove these illness claims through stealth tactics and Blackthorn Panther is just the man to do it, believes George McPullis. Naturally, Blackthorn Panther agrees.

So, just who is the mystery gentleman? Blackthorn removes his black crash helmet and hangs it over the handlebars of Wanda the Honda who is also black. He pulls out the folded, printed instructions from the inside pocket of his black leather jacket. They explain in detail the answer but strangely to Blackthorn, not until page five. He refreshes his memory and carefully reads again.

Name: Bartholomew Rupert Kingsley-Albritton. Residence: Belwain Manor, Little Belwain, Woldshire. He sounds important though Blackthorn has never heard of him. He continues reading. *Age: Seventy-Six. Height: Five Feet Six Inches., Build: Slight. Hair: Thinning Grey usually swept to right. Distinguishing Features: Distinct Scar Above Right Eye. Speaks like Royalty.* Blackthorn scans further. *It is alleged that he spends his days in a wheelchair but occasionally manages to walk with crutches in a stooped manner.*

Blackthorn grins. Stooped Manor is where he should live, not Belwain Manor. He's aware that his wry sense of humor is likely to get him into trouble one of these days. He skips through details of the location and turns to page six. His eyes are immediately drawn to the set of instructions found mid-page. They're deemed important enough to be in both bold font, capitals and to justify three exclamation marks.

GET THE PROOF WE NEED. GET HIM TO COURT!!!

This final instruction failed to add *AT ANY COST* in the opinion of Blackthorn, but he was pleased enough with the substantial down payment which will at least guarantee his rent is covered for the month.

Today is a first visit, a reconnaissance mission. He needs to figure out who and what he's up against. Kingsley-Albritton certainly seems to be a man of mystery and now a wanted man to boot.

To have avoided going to court for so long takes some doing, concludes Blackthorn. This guy knows people. He's bucking authority just because he can or truly is very ill. He could be dangerous or more likely, the people he knows will be.

What have I got myself into? He tucks the instructions back inside his jacket and with crash helmet back on, guides Wanda slowly into the village. One lady walking a black dog sums up the entire activity in Little Belwain. "Guess everyone's gone to Great Belwain," Blackthorn mutters, tongue-in-cheek.

He recalls from the instructions that it's a one road in, one road out sort of place and that Belwain Manor will be found at the far end from where he is now, on the left tucked away behind an extraordinarily high hedge and gates. Reference to a road, however, is an elaboration. It's a lane and not much of one at that. Potholes abound, some patched, many not and a continuous growth of grass and weeds define the centre line. Deep puddles lay along its sides and it's little wider than a regular car apart from an occasional purposefully created passing space.

Blackthorn vigilantly steers Wanda along the track at low speed to avoid any embarrassing slip up or, more likely, slip off. He eventually passes a gathering of old cottages and a modest detached house that architecturally suggests it may have once been a railway signal box prior to a decent enough conversion.

Several rather nice detached houses come and go. He notes that the last two are particularly large, with long sweeping drives and grass paddocks to the front. As he negotiates a double bend, the road straightens and continues up a steady incline for several hundred yards before disappearing over a ridge. He opens Wanda's throttle and she booms her approval allowing him to reach the summit in double quick time. Before bringing her to a breathtaking halt on the top of what turns out to be a bridge, it occurs to him that he's perhaps come too far and somehow missed the manor. Now that he's stopped however, all is revealed, or almost so.

Ahead on the left are chimneys, lots of them, belonging to a very grand house indeed, befitting of the name Belwain Manor and owned by Bartholomew Rupert Kingsley-Albritton, he suspects. An extremely high hedge prevents any further view of the house beyond. "Privet possibly," he guesses, but whatever it is, concealment is its purpose and it's doing a fine job.

He observes that the bridge is built of old red brick and it crosses a former railway cutting, now overgrown, that appears to skirt the Belwain Manor Estate perimeter. The grass field to his right rises steeply with several trees dotted here and there. He spies a white farmhouse and the steeple of a church in the far distance but that's about it. Belwain Manor is the perfect location for a recluse. It's literally in the middle of nowhere.

Blackthorn surveys his options before continuing over the bridge and down the hill beyond. Only when he is close to the hedge does he realize its dominating height. Sixteen feet or more of dense foliage, he estimates. It's impressive by anyone's standards. He motors along its side and past tall solid timber double gates at a sedate speed. He notices an entry system built into a stone column to the right of the gates and there are high-level cameras too. He wasn't surprised to note that a welcome sign was nowhere to be seen. Belwain Manor is most definitely not on any tourist map.

This one is going to be tricky, to say the least. Thank goodness Blackthorn Panther is the greatest living private detective of his day. About half a mile further on, the track deteriorates to such an extent as only being accessible to farm vehicles and off-roaders. He turns Wanda around and points her the way he's come.

"Seen enough," he utters confidently out loud and completes another drive past Belwain Manor before heading home.

He has some serious thinking to do.

Chapter Seven

NEXT MORNING, BLACKTHORN IS UP with the lark. He once more successfully negotiates the lane through Little Belwain and pulls Wanda in through a convenient open field entrance on the right, about one hundred yards before the old railway bridge where he'd stopped the day before. He tucks Wanda behind a hedgerow out of sight and leaves his crash helmet on her seat and under his leather jacket.

It's just seven fifteen. He jogs his way across the ever-rising field, wearing a compact khaki military rucksack on his back. At the brow of the hill, he leans against one of several trees in the vicinity to catch his breath. The view across the surrounding countryside is dramatic but he needs to get even higher as the chimneys, roof and tops of windows are the only parts of Belwain Manor currently in sight.

He seeks out the tallest tree and climbs like a panther. It's a tricky ascent as his rucksack constantly catches on branches but higher and higher he ascends until he's in the treetops and can go no further. He wedges himself between two limbs and exhales strongly. From the rucksack, he takes out a Vimto, flips open the ring-pull, takes a gulp and precariously sets it down beside him. Next to leave the rucksack is another gift from his parents, Dad this time. Nikon Field Power Opera-Sized Binoculars 7 x 20 were on Blackthorn's wish list for last Christmas and Dad had delivered.

"Thanks Dad," he whispers, as he adjusts the focus and spies in the direction of Belwain Manor. He can now see a section of the drive leading up to the front of the house, but the front door and more than half of the building is still hidden behind the tall hedge. He decides to do no more than wait in the tree for the next few hours. Someone is bound to come in or out of the gates sooner or later, he figures, but he's wrong.

Eleven o'clock comes and goes and the tree isn't the only one with stiff limbs on the top of a hill overlooking Belwain Manor, and now it's beginning to rain. Blackthorn feels out of luck and decides on another tactic. He moves to start his descent and promptly knocks the Vimto can out of the tree. The tiny Nikon binoculars join his Nikon camera in the rucksack and down he clambers, but it's more difficult coming down than it was going up. Eventually, after several close accidental attempts to imitate the Vimto can, he returns to terra firma, pops the empty can into the rucksack, throws it onto his back and sets off across the field towards the old railway cutting.

Down into the cutting he scrambles and makes his way in the direction of the bridge, stumbling on a multitude of obstacles hidden in the undergrowth. Under the bridge he advances, grateful that the rain has now stopped. The next few hundred yards is slow going as there is so much debris underfoot and he does well to avoid twisting an ankle or worse. He congratulates himself on reaching the point where the cutting veers away to the left without minor or serious injury, crawling out to rest in the long grass at the top of the bank.

The trek is worth it. Without the high roadside hedge for concealment, Belwain Manor stands before him in all her glory, albeit still around quarter of a mile away. His binoculars do their job in noticing detail for the first time. Three stories of windows with more dormers in the grey steeply banked roof. He counts five tall chimneys, each with six pots. It's a large stone building, possibly limestone but impossible to tell from this distance and in the Palladian style, notes Blackthorn, recalling his architecture classes from way back when, details none of which are of primary importance right now. The large single, black front door is accessed by a bank of steps and he can see it clearly through the Nikon lens. He can't see any vehicles though or anybody for that matter. The entire place could well be deserted. The long grass is wet from the recent shower and Blackthorn is lying prostrate in it, sniper-like. He's trying to decide for how long he's going to stay, when bingo! There's movement. Someone has just come out through the front door and walks hurriedly across the pebbled courtyard area, heading towards an outbuilding which Blackthorn observes has a red-tiled roof. The figure disappears from view. He believes it to be a man but doesn't get a camera shot to prove or disprove his theory. I'll get him when he goes back in, he promises himself.

Being a successful Private Investigator requires patience, oodles of it. Blackthorn Panther is learning this on almost every case. Hours of boredom interspersed with sudden action that you must be ready to act upon in an instant. This figure's sudden appearance has caught him off-guard, and that's another lesson learned. Forty minutes pass before Blackthorn sees the figure retracing its steps back towards the house. Readily prepared this time, he snaps away. Definitely a man. He walks with a normal gait with no obvious sign of infirmity or difficulty. He enters the door and Blackthorn decides that it's time to leave.

To avoid detection, he slides down the embankment back into the cutting and makes his way cautiously again along the track, under the bridge and up into the field beyond. What he sees next is both unexpected and alarming. There is a large blue tractor stopped alongside Wanda and a Police minivan complete with flashing blue light on its roof is parked in the lane. Blackthorn notices a large policeman in uniform holding his leather jacket in the air seemingly ready for inspection. He's talking with an agricultural gentleman and Blackthorn sprints down the field towards them.

As he nears, he hears the policeman say, "I guess that'll be the culprit." He's pointing at Blackthorn as both men stare him down.

"Hello, gents," he shouts, still thirty feet away. "Is there a problem?"

"There might be, and there might not be," says the policeman seriously. "Does this 'ere motorcycle belong to you?"

"Absolutely she does, Officer. Isn't she a beauty?" Blackthorn's brain is working overtime. "I'm so sorry I had to leave her here. He turns to face the ruddy-faced tractor driver as he stands Wanda upright. "And so sorry sir for any inconvenience to you. I had an emergency you see."

Before he can continue, the policeman taps him on the right shoulder and adds, "And what sort of emergency would that be, young man?"

Blackthorn doesn't miss a beat.

"An extremely urgent one, Officer." He disengages from his rucksack and delves inside. The two men look on inquisitively. Blackthorn takes a moment to rummage around and produces, a roll of toilet paper! He holds it triumphantly aloft.

"Bloody curries," he lies. He repossesses his jacket from the grimacing policeman before even he realizes it. He addresses both men while donning his crash helmet and getting astride Wanda. "It's been a pleasure to meet you both. Thank you for all you do, Officer, in keeping us safe from villains, and to you, sir, for your wonderful," he hesitates, "all your wonderful farming," he finishes gleefully. Wanda fires up, and before he's even asked to produce his driving license, he's off. He glances into his rearview mirror to see the two men standing in the middle of the lane, hands on hips, soon to be scratching their heads, no doubt.

Blackthorn phews loudly into his visor and offers a high, engaging wave. "And never forget to take toilet roll with you when out on surveillance," had been Dad's advice. And not for the first time, Dad was right again.

Chapter Eight

I T IS EVIDENT THAT BLACKTHORN MUST GAIN access into Belwain Manor to confront Bartholomew Rupert Kingsley-Albritton in person. There is likely no other way to obtain the evidence required. He needs a dose of inspiration and what better way than a night on the tiles with his good friend, Rob. It's early evening and Blackthorn is sitting alone in his apartment, as usual. He's had a few girlfriends, even a broken off engagement once upon a time, but was happily single right now, sort of. He recalls that there is a fancy-dress event tonight at The Miss Ritzy Nightclub in town, and phones Rob to see if he fancies going. Rob picks up straightaway and is at a loose end himself. He jumps at the chance of enjoying a few bevvies with his friend. They discuss options on what costumes to wear and arrange to meet at nine thirty outside the club and to surprise each other.

Being a Private Investigator does tend to ensure punctuality and at precisely nine thirty, Blackthorn is standing outside the nightclub. He has had an eventful day. Now is the time to let his hair down and what better way to do it than by going to a nightclub dressed as a wolf!

He'd dashed to Party Costumes for All and arrived just as they were ready to close. The girl in the shop was about to turn the open sign to closed when he almost fell in. He had pleaded with her to let him choose something unusual because he was going to an amazing party. He'd given her his best Blackthorn smile and she had relented, giving him just a minute or two to make his choice. She was going out on a hot date and couldn't be late, even for him.

He stood there, eyes dancing from one rack of outfits to another. He had absolutely no idea. Moments later, she had handed over a large polythene bag, taken ten pounds off him and told him to return it without fail in the morning. Before he knew it, he was out the door, so was she, and the shop was locked and in darkness. She was gone into the night. He'd got back home and there discovered her choice for him. Having tried it on, he discovered it fit perfectly but boy, it was warm. It had a large convenient pocket inside where he could carry some cash and his apartment key.

He sets off on the thirty-minute walk for his rendezvous with Rob. He ignores the car honks and funny comments along the way and now here he is, at nine thirty-five, standing outside The Miss Ritzy Nightclub in full wolf attire. This includes the largest wolf head known to mankind.

A few clubbers pass him and enter the club. They give him funny glances and so does the doorman. They've not even bothered to get dressed up, he observes critically. They should at least get into the swing of things and now here's Rob.

"Poor effort," he calls to Rob who approaches wearing what he normally wears, except for the addition of a vicar's white dog collar. Blackthorn splutters. "I think I've definitely won the award for best costume. Let me reassure you, though, mate. You'll probably come second. I've seen people going in and they've not bothered to get dressed up at all! Feeble effort if you ask me."

Rob is speechless. He can't stop staring at the talking, hairy grey wolf standing before him, complete with an open mouth, revealing sharp rubber white teeth and a long red material tongue that falls out its side.

"You've surpassed yourself this time, Blacky," he says, shaking his head. "I didn't know it was you until I heard your voice."

Blackthorn asks him to complete the zip operation at the back of the costume which he couldn't reach himself earlier, and once done, they're ready to get this show on the road. The Wolf and the Vicar go to enter the club, but the doorman raises his arm like a policeman stopping traffic.

"And where do you think you're going, ladies?'

Blackthorn hates a lack of respect and gives the stockily-built skinhead doorman his most fierce Panther look, which he can't see of course because of the giant wolf head.

"Is there any reason on this planet why we can't go in?" Blackthorn is determined. "Please don't force me to huff and puff and blow your nightclub down." Rob remains calm and impressed. The doorman looks them both up and down, then repeats the act.

"I guess not," he snorts. The hard guy slightly titters like a little girl and drops his arm. "Have a good night, gents."

The two make their way through open double doors and reach a large desk coupled to a fairground-type of turnstile. An older lady takes their entry money and doesn't bat an eyelid. As they move into the darkness of the club, she calls back to them, "You do know the fancy dress got changed to next week, don't you dears?" Blackthorn comes to an abrupt halt. He hopes the floor will open up and swallow him whole. He turns and looks at the lady.

"You're kidding, right?"

She puts her hand horizontally to her face and moves it up and down. "Do I look like I'm kidding?" She shakes her head in disbelief but quickly gets on with accepting money from a line of other clubbers, all dressed in normal clubbing gear.

"Shit," blurts Blackthorn.

"No problem," says Rob who whips off his dog collar in two seconds flat and stuffs it into a pocket.

They stand motionless and stare at each other though Rob is unaware that Blackthorn is staring— Blackthorn being the person who cannot be seen. They're both contemplating the same thing. Should they stay, or should they go? Blackthorn is resolute. "I've hired this outfit. We're in the club and we're going to have a great time, and you're buying the first drinks." Rob has much admiration for his friend, reaches into his pocket and puts the dog collar back on.

"We're in this together," he laughs and they both stride off towards the nearest bar, one of them with his tail between his legs.

Miss Ritzy Nightclub has a large circular rotating bar, the talk of the town, you might say. The two intrepid heroes get their drinks and lean against the bar, surveying the dance floor. The club is probably less than a quarter full, but a steady stream of people is now entering as the pubs in town begin to close their doors.

By eleven o'clock, the place is bustling. Blondie, The Boomtown Rats and some other dance music unfamiliar to Blackthorn booms away and the temperature inside the wolf outfit is reaching boiling point.

Blackthorn is a trooper and remains in good spirits and full wolf attire, despite having to consume his pints of draught beer through a straw and receiving a battery of comments; "Are you a girl or a guy in there?" "Are you a sheep in wolf's clothing?" "Give us a howl!" Several of the nicer remarks politely inform him that the fancy dress is now next week. "I know," replies Blackthorn. "I'm coming as a human then."

Now he needs to go to the men's room and Rob has wandered off and is nowhere to be seen. Blackthorn makes his way over to a far corner where two lines of customers are awaiting their turn to use the facilities. The line for guys has just four in it, waiting patiently outside the entry door and the ladies about five hundred—or fifteen, to be more accurate. He needs to go and quickly. He fights to reach the zip but to no avail. It's out of reach. Stupid costume. How on earth are you supposed to get out of it once you're in it? He is suddenly in desperate straits.

"Hi, you okay Mr. Wolfman?"

He turns to face the most beautiful she-wolf he has ever laid eyes on! She is gorgeous, and Blackthorn is instantly smitten. Her big brown eyes with whites like snow pierce his costume like a cupid's arrow and her brunette, tousled hair perfectly frames her even more perfect face. He's in wolf dreamland and considers howling out loud but his desperation to urinate is all consuming. She's next in her line and he's fourth in his.

He comes to his senses just in time. "Please, any chance of unzipping me?" He indicates vaguely in the direction of the zip at the back. "I guess if I'd come as an orangutan, I'd be able to reach it myself." She giggles a sweet giggle that plays music in his heart.

"I thought you'd never ask," and with the deed done and those words melting into his wolf ears, she is gone through the door to the ladies. Just a minute or two later, he arrives at his destination and the relief is beyond measure.

He pushes against the swing door and he's back in the club. He needs to find Rob. He edges his way past those standing in lines and there she is, positioned directly in his way. He inches towards her and stops close. Very close.

"I thought you'd need zipping back up again." Gorgeous and thoughtful.

"Absolutely." Mister I-can-think-of-anything-to-say-at-any-time-in-an-instant, is dumbstruck. She turns him around by placing hands on both shoulders and completes the zip operation.

"Aren't you hot inside there?"

"It's like a furnace," replies Blackthorn and she giggles that gorgeous giggle again.

"Why not take it off?" she suggests.

"I only have underwear underneath," he replies, "and I'm totally naked under that." She smiles a smile that Blackthorn reckons would melt an ice cap.

"Just the head, silly. Just the head." And off it comes, inch by inch until suffocation by wolf costume is a thing of the past and death attributed to heat exhaustion is averted by mere seconds. That's two huge amounts of relief in the last thirty seconds or so for Blackthorn. He feels slightly subconscious about the beads of sweat trickling down his face and his hair pasted to his head as though dunked in a bucket of water.

She reassures him. "Kinda cute," she giggles. "Who are you with?" Blackthorn barely remembers.

"My mate's here somewhere," says Blackthorn, looking around and seeing a Rob-less crowd. He thinks he may not at this instant notice Rob if he came along and stood nose to nose! He looks back at his newfound companion. Their eyes meet, and fireworks explode in his head. "You do know the fancy dress thing is next week now, don't you?"

"I only found out when I got here," Blackthorn says in a resigned tone.

"I'm thirsty," she says, moving on quickly. "Can I get you a bowl of water maybe or perhaps some reindeer blood or whatever it is that wolves drink when they go clubbing?" Off they head to the rotating bar.

She's talking and despite the loud music, he's listening. Time stands still for Blackthorn. The wolf head sits on the bar. He learns that she's recently graduated from Swanton University and now lives in nearby

Lechford with her parents. She's considering plans to travel around the world before getting a job but has decided to just take some time out to enjoy herself. Blackthorn is happy to hear this angel talk all night.

A voice appears out of the darkness. Rob has turned up. "Where have you been? I've been looking everywhere for you." He does a double take. "And to whom do I have the pleasure?" he continues. Blackthorn's dazzling new friend introduces herself to them both.

"I'm Charli," she reports. "It's short for Charlotte but my friends call me Charli—Charli without an e." Rob completes a lingering study. She's wearing a sparkly short silver dress with matching, sparkly, short-heeled silver shoes. She holds a small silver clutch bag and looks simply wonderful! Her tanned smooth skin radiates warmth. She possesses the prettiest of faces, observes Rob, and she's hooking up with his sweaty best friend Blackthorn, who's come dressed as a wolf.

How is this even remotely possible? He places one hand on Blackthorn's shoulder and pats it approvingly. He offers the other to Charli and they shake hands. He pulls her hand towards him and effortlessly rolls it over, leans forward and plants it with a kiss. Very Prince Charming, worries Blackthorn.

"Well Miss Charli without an e. Any friend of Blacky's is a friend of mine." He seems happy and turns to half-face Blackthorn. "I've met someone, Blacky.

Hope we can catch up in an hour or so, or later in the week." He winks a mischievous wink and hugs his drinking buddy. "By the way, you look better with the wolf head on," he laughs before heading off into the dance floor throng and moments later, he's gone.

"I don't agree. You have amazing features, Blacky." She holds her hand softly against the side of his face and allows her fingers to fall slowly down his cheek and tip-toe across his jawline. They brush his lips.

"I can call you Blacky, can't I?" He is inwardly praying for this moment never to end. He manages the slightest of nods as the trance is broken. "So, Mr. Blacky Wolf," she says playfully. "Tell me what Blacky is short for?"

He temporarily regains his senses. "Blackthorn, like the cider." She looks intently at him, he thinks to gauge whether he's being truthful. "Really," he confirms. "It's true. My name is Blackthorn. Blackthorn Panther. You can't make it up."

She licks those delicious lips and leans into him. He can almost feel her beautiful fit body against his, but the thick wolf outfit prevents total sensory emersion. She whispers in his ear. "My favourite new drink by far."

He thinks he's just died and gone to heaven. "I'm leaving now but call me, Mr. Blackthorn Panther." She turns away momentarily and easily manages to gain the immediate attention of one of the guys working the bar, who grabs her a pen and a scrap of paper.

She scribbles away and hands Blackthorn the tiny note. It has a telephone number on it. She tugs at the hairy wolf chest and pulls him closer, depositing a kiss on each cheek, then one full on the lips for good measure. It's a quick kiss but has Blackthorn floating on air. Seconds later, she too is gone.

One more perusal from his elevated position at the bar fails to locate Rob. He leaves, wolf head tucked awkwardly under his arm and gets a renewed cluster of drunken comments and jeers on his way. The thug-looking doorman is still there and has been joined by a similar-looking colleague. The new guy points with disdain and begins to laugh but the first one stops him abruptly with an air swipe of a muscular arm. "You're a good sport, kid. Most would've gone home. Fair play to you." His friendly tone is unexpected which warms Blackthorn as he begins the long walk home. "See you next week," calls out his new door-man friend but he is barely heard.

Blackthorn can't get Charli off his mind and de-spite the weight of the sweat-soaked outfit and the late hour, finds himself skipping his way back to the apartment. The skipping wolf holds tightly on to the piece of paper as though his life depends upon it. What a girl and what a night!

Chapter Nine

FIRST TASK OF THE DAY IS TO RETURN the wolf outfit. He carries it in the bag supplied and drops it off at the shop. The female assistant, a different one from the night before, is gleeful to see it.

"We've had that in for nearly a month and you're the first to choose it. I thought no-one would pick that." She exudes astonishment. Blackthorn is quietly comforted in the knowledge that no-one else before him had sweated through a party or done anything else in it, for that matter. "It was perfect, actually," he replies. "Absolutely perfect." He's recalling his encounter with Charli, as she likes to call herself. He considers telling the shop girl that he didn't make the choice at all, and that it was all the doing of her late-shift colleague, but it seems trivial and he chooses to keep silent.

He has lunch at The Black Bull, consisting of a salad buffet accompanied by a delicious gooey French bread pizza. He sets his sights in the afternoon on formulating a plan to get inside Belwain Manor, but he's still struggling to come up with an idea. He can't seem to get negative thoughts out of his head. This guy is going to be extremely wary. There is absolutely no way that Kingsley-Albritton is going to readily let anyone through his gates, never mind into his home and allow photographs to be taken. So just what to do? Blackthorn has concluded that he gets some of his best ideas when riding Wanda, so he takes her out for a spin and waits for the genius within to emerge.

He rides out of town and heads for the hills. In thirty minutes, he's enjoying panoramic views from The Trackway Downs, a ridge of hills that dominate the surrounding landscape. Swinborough is visible on the horizon but there is not another soul around, except for a couple hiking about a quarter of a mile to the west. He spots cars moving along distant roads, akin to toys. It's a warm late summer afternoon and he enjoys the peaceful solitude. He sits with elbows on thighs and chin resting between clenched fists. This seems to be the perfect thinking spot. He gazes dreamily and waits for inspiration to arrive. When none does, he recalls the events of the night before, of meeting Charli and the crumpled piece of paper now lying on his kitchen countertop. He decides then and there that, when he gets home, he'll call her, but before that he takes some scenic photos.

He takes a short detour on the way home and heads for Stratley, an area of north Swinborough and home to his good friend, Pete Briggenssen, who is a Danish national. He works at a local car dealership but, more importantly to Blackthorn, is a photography enthusiast. He has his own darkroom at home and often develops Blackthorn's films in exchange for a couple of beers now and again. Blackthorn rings the doorbell multiple times before Pete appears. "Hey there. Were you in the back developing?"

Pete looks disheveled as though he's just woken up or been wrestling a tiger. "You could say that. Say hi, Inga." Around his shoulder pops a pretty, little face framed by lots of blonde hair.

Blackthorn praises himself. Wrestling a tigress. Close guess. These two have been close friends for ages but Pete has continually stressed that there was nothing physical between them. Blackthorn reasons that the playing field has now been somewhat altered.

"Hi Blacky," says Inga as instructed, and with that she disappears back into Pete's dinky cottage. "Good for you. Good for both of you," congratulates Blackthorn. "It's about time you made a dishonest woman of her." The two guys hug on the doorstep.

"I'll not come in seeing as you're busy," Blackthorn grins, "but would appreciate you developing this film for me. It's pretty urgent, actually." He hands over the film and Pete smiles. Pete always smiles.

"Sure thing, Blacky. I'll get on it later tonight and it'll be ready for you in the morning." Pete has never let Blackthorn down. Not only is he an enthusiast but also an absolute perfectionist and has never once missed an agreed deadline.

"Brilliant, my friend. I'll drop by before ten. Congrats again. I think you're perfect for one another." He turns to leave when loud music stops him in his tracks. Inga reappears in the doorway wearing not much, balancing a monstrous silver radio on her left shoulder. "I got it yesterday, Blacky. It's a boom box. Don't you just love it?" At that moment, the latest song from Olivia Newton-John starts playing. The three friends listen together.

"A place where nobody dared to go, the love that we came to know, they call it Xanadu."

A light bulb flashes inside Blackthorn's head. He takes three strides towards Inga and places a huge kiss on her forehead. "Thanks Inga. You're a star. See you tomorrow, Pete," and with that, he was back on Wanda and heading for home.

During the ride, he keeps singing the opening lines of the song he's just heard. He gets strange looks from pedestrians at traffic lights and a few smiles too. One elderly lady even joins in.

He leaves Wanda in her allocated parking space and dashes up to the apartment. He writes down the song lyrics in his tiny notebook. It's as though a great fog has lifted. At last he has an idea. He continues writing and reads out loud, "Bartholomew Rupert Kingsley-Albritton. Your days are numbered. Thank you, Pete, Inga and last, but not least, Olivia Newton-John, for your inspiration." He retrieves the Charli note from the kitchen and manages to straighten it out with his hand sufficient to make out the numbers. He goes over to his phone and notices that Ellen has been at work in his absence.

There are again three messages. He goes through them, pen poised to make any required notes. Message one is from Mum. "You haven't called me yet, son. Hope you got my message the other day. I don't like these machines you know. Call me. I need to know you're alright. Love you. Bye. Oh, I've got a new recipe for you, but I think I told you that already. Okay, bye."

He writes, *Call Mum.*

Message two is very formal. "Reginald Smith here representing Messrs. Allday, Crabham, Wallenhurst and Bentham. You will recall that we are expecting an interim report on the Kingsley-Albritton case within the next few days. Please ensure that we receive it in a timely manner. We do not, I repeat do not, expect to chase you up on this matter. The contract is clear. Should you fail to supply interim reports, your contract will be terminated immediately. Trust that is clear. We collectively thank you for your services thus far."

If he added anything else, too bad. Ellen ended the message for him. He again writes: *Interim Report to Complete by Friday.*

Message number three. He hopes it will be short, so he can get on with calling Charli. "Hello there, Mr. Real Panther camouflaged as a wolf. I love your answering message, by the way. You probably won't remember me, but we met at Ritzy's last night. I had a great time and just wanted to check up to see you got home okay. The name's Charli. Call me if you want to. Oh, by the way, I found your number in the phone directory. Hope you don't mind."

He stands and walks to the kitchen. "I'll call you in around forty-five minutes," he asserts out loud. He nonchalantly paces around the room precisely three times, then leaps for the phone.

Chapter Ten

BLACKTHORN LISTENS PATIENTLY. The ringing seems to go on forever. He envisages Charli's mum picking up and the two of them having a Sylvia's Mother by Dr. Hook sort of conversation. He considers hanging up when at last there's an answer. He needn't have worried.

"Hello, who's that?" He immediately recognizes the sweet voice though she sounds out of breath. He readies himself by inhaling slightly. "It's Blackthorn here. From last ..." She interrupts before he can finish. "Blacky Wolfman Panther. Where have you been all my life? Sorry it took so long to get to the phone. We're all out in the garden and I had to run to get it." She takes a deep breath. "I sort of hoped it would be you." Blackthorn gives himself a surprised kind of smile. "Are you still there?" she asks.

"Absolutely yes." He finds himself nodding.

"I'm still here. So, how are you?" He winces. Really! Is that my best line?

She chooses not to let the lack of an intelligent question come between them. "I'm great, thanks."

Blackthorn blurts, "Yes, you are," then immediately regrets it, and gets down to business. "Look, Charli, I need to let you in on something." His tone is serious.

"Intrigue. I love it," she responds without any hesitation. He continues, "I'm a private investigator and I have a really interesting case going on right now."

"That sounds amazing, Blacky. You're not investigating me, are you?" He laughs. "I wish. I'll leave that to another day. No, but I do have a proposal for you."

"Wow! You're fast off the mark, even for a Panther," she giggles.

Blackthorn fleetingly contemplates asking her to marry him then and there but quickly and for the sake of them both, comes to his senses. He's back to the reason for his call.

"No, no, not that sort of proposal. You are too cheeky by half. Fact is, I think you'll have a lot of fun on this case and we'll make a great team. Do you happen to have any stuff from university?" For once, there's a slight pause at the end of the line.

"So, let me get this straight, Mr. Blackthorn Panther, PI. You just want me for some illicit gain. Is that your evil plan?"

He's unsure whether she's being playful again or not. "Not illicit. Just, well …" He's trying to figure out the right words but thankfully, she puts him out of his misery.

"I'm kidding. I'd love to, Blacky, and I have lots of uni stuff. Tell me what you need, and I'll get it. I'm your girl." He says "I wish" for a second time but only in his head.

"Are you free tomorrow? I know it's short notice, but this case waits for no man, or woman for that matter. There's a place, where nobody dares to go, they call it Xanadu," he adds in the worst out-of-tune rendition of that song, ever.

"Free as a bird and I love Olivia Newton-John. I'll be ready whenever you want, and I'll have some uni stuff ready for you."

"Great. I'll see you at ten thirty in the morning." She gives him an address in Lechford and some simple directions.

"Bye, bye Blacky. See you soon, and Xanadu of course." she finishes enthusiastically and hangs up. Blackthorn's master plan has started perfectly.

As a new day dawns, Blackthorn is one busy PI. Before he leaves the apartment, he steps into the bathroom and checks his image in the large mirror. Blue casual shirt to match his eyes, blue jeans and black Dr.

Martens boots, always his go-to comfy choice when likely to be on his feet all day. He decides to add to the expense account for this case and rides Wanda down to Beat Ups Beat Down where he temporarily exchanges her for a Fiat 127 that he is assured is reliable, apart from the times when it breaks down. He is surprised to learn that Mr. Volvo was booked out and unavailable. "I'm not their only customer after all."

The Fiat is a dainty little thing and not a vehicle designed for a high-speed chase but is perfect for what lay ahead. It's light grass-green color will blend in perfectly in a countryside full of multiple shades of green, he jokes. He places his trusty rucksack on the back seat and heads off for Pete's to collect his photographs.

Pete answers the door almost immediately without Inga distractions to delay him. "Glad you're early, Blacky. They need me in the dealership at noon." He hands over the photos without an envelope.

"You know me, mate. Never late. Let's catch up at the weekend if you're free."

Pete agrees and moments later, Blackthorn is heading for Lechford. He's making great time and fears being way too early for Charli. His journey takes him through the small town of Highfield Wick where he pulls into one of the marked-out street parking spaces outside The White Lion Tavern. The Fiat is silenced. He begins to examine the photographs and flips through them quickly before focusing on those of the person he'd seen outside

Belwain Manor. He is ninety-nine percent certain that it's a man simply by the walk. He's wearing green corduroy jeans with a green and brown check jacket and a flat cap. He's of slight build but that's all he can make out with any degree of certainty. "Insufficient evidence," he mutters. "Careful Bartholomew, I'm coming to get you."

With that, he turns the ignition key and the little Fiat does precisely nothing, except make a clunking sound. He tries again with the same result. "Please, please, please don't do this," pleads Blackthorn. He counts to three and tries again. Still nothing except another clunk. He gets out and after some difficulty in accessing the engine compartment, gives a half-decent impression of a car mechanic.

He prods and pokes he knows not what. Just about the only thing he recognizes is an oil dipstick. He recalls an expression his dad uses often for when he has no idea about a subject. "Yes Dad, I am totally flummoxed." He immediately recalls another Dad saying. "If in doubt, give it a clout." Blackthorn deduces that he has inherited his dad's mechanical expertise and follows the adage nothing ventured, nothing gained. He gives just about everything he can see a good clobbering with the sole of his size ten Dr. Martens. Moments later, he's back in and turns the ignition key, more in hope than expectation. The Fiat miraculously bursts into life. He thanks his dad out loud while looking to heaven, even though Dad is at home in

Tellingford, and begins the last five miles or so of his trip to pick up Charli.

The directions are simple enough and he pulls up outside a large detached house built from Cotsdean Stone. Habit kicks in and he unintentionally turns off the Fiat engine. He hopes not to regret the deed. The house is set back from the road and the immaculate lawns to the front are substantial. A cobble-stoned circular drive cuts a divide through the grass and a black Range Rover is parked close to the front door, which swings open before he's even halfway towards it. Charli bounds out and greets him like a recruit returning home after a long campaign overseas, throwing her arms around his neck and giving him a hug to end all hugs.

Did I really meet this girl for the first time just two nights ago? he questions himself. "Good to see you too," Blackthorn says as he untangles himself.

"I've got everything you want," she claims. Why does she keep saying these things? She dashes back to the front door and grabs a Swanton University scarf that she holds aloft.

"It's a bit warm for that, Charli." He's feeling particularly hot under the collar right now. She's wearing a white T-shirt sporting a Swanton University emblem that clings perfectly to where it should and a flowery, thin fabric mid-length skirt with brown leather cowgirl style boots that complete her outfit.

She displays all manner of things from her former university. Blackthorn focuses on those proudly displaying the Swanton University logo and decides it won't hurt to bring the lot.

"So, whose car are we going in, Blacky? Yours or mine?" She's looking over at the gleaming Range Rover. He glances back at the decrepit beat up Fiat that probably has less than a fifty percent chance of even starting, never mind getting them both safely all the way to Little Belwain and back.

"Shouldn't we ask your parents first? I mean, shouldn't I be meeting them first?" She looks at him with a smile. "You're such a gentleman, Blacky. "They're not even here. They left early this morning to go see friends in London. The car is mine, a gift for excelling at uni."

Just over an hour later, they pass the sign indicating the periphery of Little Belwain. They're in the Fiat. He had kept his fingers crossed and silently prayed as he had turned the ignition key. He hadn't been let down. He'd reminded Charli that this was an undercover operation and the Range Rover would be far too conspicuous. During the journey, he'd explained the plan, that Xanadu is really Belwain Manor and he plans to ensure that love is his target's downfall.

Charli can hardly contain her excitement. She's a clever little thing herself but credits Blackthorn with genius status for his idea. Moments later, they begin the next phase of the plan which is to be in Little Belwain for legitimate reasons for as long as possible and to see what they can find out about the manor and its reclusive owner.

Chapter Eleven

ALF A DAY IS SPENT VISITING EVERY HOME in Little Belwain. Their ruse is that they are students from Swanton University working on a thesis covering rural architecture and history. They speak with as many of the residents as they possibly can, collecting and recording information in their Swanton notebooks. No suspicion is aroused. They look the part and play it to perfection. They speak with one lady of retirement age who, astonishingly, tells them that she has lived in the same house her entire life. She had cleaned inside the manor for the previous owners, David and Louise Whittington, who she described as just lovely genuine people, but when they'd sold about five years ago, her position working there went with them. The new owner had blatantly refused to re-hire and was immediately known to her henceforth as a mean old bugger.

Throughout their house visits, they learn that Kingsley-Albritton has a reputation of keeping himself to himself and never involves himself in local affairs, much to the chagrin of almost every local.

At last, they reach the two larger homes Blackthorn had observed on his previous visits. The first of the two is a damp squib. No one at home. The second one is a different story. There's a white Ford Transit parked on the drive alongside a green Ford Granada. The Transit has ladders on its roof and on its side, the words "The Belwain Painting Company." A local telephone number is listed. "Looks like someone has the decorators in," Blackthorn suggests to Charli.

She has been such a help to Blackthorn so far, having managed to totally charm details from even those on their doorsteps that were at first reluctant or just plain annoyed that anyone should dare to have the audacity to knock or ring a doorbell in Little Belwain. Such things just don't happen here!

A tall, thin man opens the door. Blackthorn estimates his age to be around fifty. "Excuse me, sir," begins Blackthorn.

"And what can I do for you two?" he interrupts. He's addressing them both but staring only in Charli's direction. Blackthorn knows exactly how he feels. Charli takes over. Charli almost always takes over.

"I've some painting that needs doing and I saw the van." Blackthorn gives her a glance. She laughs and pokes the thin guy on the shoulder. He's smiling too.

"Only joking," she reveals. "We're doing this thesis you see and would like to ask you a few questions about what it's like living in Little Belwain, what made you buy in this location and what you like best about your house? Things like that, but if you've got the decorators in right now, my friend here," she nods in the direction of Blackthorn, "can come back on his own another time." The man looks Charli up and down. Guys have a habit of doing that, Blackthorn has noticed.

"Then if this is a one-time only visit by yourself, I'd better answer all your questions today, young lady," he replies light-heartedly. "And I always have the decorators in, as I'm the decorator." Blackthorn doesn't feel the need to get involved too much. Charli has got this.

"Okay, Mr. Wonderful Belwain Painting Company Man," and she proceeds to ask all the agreed questions and he gives up all the answers obediently, as though under a spell. It's Blackthorn's turn, at last. "Thank you for your help Mister …" he hesitates expectantly, waiting for a response.

He gets one.

"Michael Twinner." He turns again to face Charli. "Mike to my friends," he adds.

Blackthorn continues. "Well, Mike. You're the last house in the village and …" He's cut short not for the first time by Mike.

"It's a hamlet, not a village," he corrects.

"Yes, a hamlet. We're both grateful for your help today. It's a shame there isn't also a large historic property around here, though. That would have been awesome for our thesis."

"But there is," says Mike enthusiastically. "Belwain Manor is along the lane a bit further. You'll go up a hill, over a bridge and you'll see it or rather you won't see it on the left. It's set back behind an extremely tall hedge, you see."

"The owner probably wouldn't want to see us though, right?" Charli sounds mournful and looks sadness personified.

Mike moves forward from his doorstep for the first time and puts his left arm lightly around Charli's shoulders. He looks to Blackthorn for approval and receives a forced smile in return. "He can be a bit of an odd-bod sometimes up there at the manor, but he's always done right by me."

Blackthorn looks over at Mike in a whole new light but it's Charli that reignites the conversation. "You know him?' she asks incredulously, breaking away from Mike and facing him like a gunslinger might. Well, she is wearing cowgirl boots!

"I've done work up there for him, yes. About a year ago, I painted almost the entire inside. Took me nearly six weeks to complete, it did. "Barty," he hesitates, and continues with an obvious adjustment. "Mr. Kingsley-Albritton is a good man. He expects a first-class job and pays well."

Charli turns to Blackthorn and raises her eyebrows as if to indicate that they may just have struck gold. Mike goes on to explain that he will put in a call to Mr. Kingsley-Albritton and ask if he will allow them access. Charli moves closer to Mike. Her hand is now on his forearm.

"Please let him know that we're very good friends of yours, won't you? My parents own a big house too and I guess it's going to need painting one day."

With that, she kisses him on the cheek and Blackthorn hands over Charli's prepared telephone number. There was no way he could risk Mike calling anyone but Charli. Imagine Mike listening to Ellen, discovering that Blackthorn was really a PI.

"Thanks Mike. When can we expect the call?"

"I'll try to get hold of him later and let you know one way or the other. I'm a man of my word."

Charli also thanks Mike in her sweetest voice, squeezes his arm and joins Blackthorn heading back to the Fiat.

Blackthorn heads them towards Belwain Manor and stops at the apex of the old railway bridge as he had done previously on Wanda. There is no traffic around. All is still. He indicates to Charli the large house beyond the hedge.

"Well, how did we do?" she eventually asks.

"Okay, I guess," teases Blackthorn. "At last, the stroke of luck we need to push the master plan forward. Thanks, Charli. You were wonderful." She smiles a grateful smile, leans across and they briefly hug.

"I guess we just need Mike to come up trumps and all will be well with the world," she adds.

"Not quite," cautions Blackthorn. "There's still plenty of work to do, but we've had a great day. Let's get you back home, but first, can I buy you a drink? I think it's my turn."

"You surely can, Blacky Wolfman, PI. Let's head for The Pike just outside Lechford. They have a pretty beer garden there down by the river, and serve a great Ploughman's Lunch," and off they set.

Blackthorn feels fortunate right now. Well, they do say fortune favors the brave. Firstly, meeting the beautiful, clever and outgoing Charli and secondly with the unexpected help from Michael Twinner, he senses at last that he is on the cusp of getting a grip on this case.

He spends an idyllic couple of hours at The Pike with Charli and learns much more about her, including her full name, Charlotte Wentworth-Kent, schools attended, university life and aspirations for the future.

They share a substantial ploughman's before returning her home. Before he leaves, she runs inside and checks for answer-machine incoming messages, specifically from Mike Twinner. Alas, there is only one from her parents who have decided to stay in London overnight. Charli promises to call Blackthorn if and when she hears from Mike.

It's early evening and he needs to urgently return the hire car. He reluctantly leaves Charli on the doorstep and gets inside the Fiat. Dismally, the thing doesn't start. A familiar clunking sound is heard.

"Problem?" calls Charli.

Blackthorn detects an opportunity to impress. "Probably, these seventy-two Fiats can be unpredictable, or so I've heard." He portrays a confidence befitting someone who knows what they're talking about. "Do me a favor. Come get into the driver's seat. When I say, turn the ignition key, go for it."

Charli duly gets herself seated and with Blackthorn bent over the engine compartment, she waits patiently for the command. Blackthorn begins his detailed engine fault analysis by crossing his fingers and delivering a silent prayer. He proceeds to fiddle around for about a minute before administering a side-hand thump to almost everything within reach. "Try her now," he calls. To his relief, the Fiat sparks again into life.

"Wow, a top mechanic too!" proclaims Charli. "A man of many talents."

"Yes," agrees Blackthorn, "though most of them hidden." They both laugh for a moment, hug for a slightly longer moment and exchange a brief kiss. He gets the Fiat rolling and Charli fast walks alongside his open window.

"I'll call you when I hear, Blacky," she chimes, and offers a short hand wave as he turns the corner and heads out of sight back towards Swinborough. He gets back to Beats Up Beat Down just minutes before they close at eight and returns the Fiat. He makes a polite request not to be offered the same car again, even though it did make him look good—for a moment or two at least.

Chapter Twelve

BACK IN HIS APARTMENT, BLACKTHORN prepares his interim report for the London lawyers and moments after its completion, the phone rings. "Hey Blacky. Guess what?" But she doesn't give him time to guess. "Mike Twinner called and we're on!" She sounds beyond excited.

"Wow! That was easier than expected," responds Blackthorn.

She continues, "Not really. Mike told me that Kingsley-Albritton refused initially. Mike then made up a story that I'm his favourite niece and this thesis is imperative to my studies. He still only agreed we could go when Mike added that I'm also a part-time model, and you're my photographer, and that I'm desperate to do some country estate shots for my portfolio."

Blackthorn senses an unease in the situation but deep down knows that this new move adds credence to his Xanadu plan to get them inside Belwain Manor. "Mike's inventive. I'll give him that," mutters Blackthorn almost inaudibly.

Charli's sensitive side reaches out. "Everything will be fine, Blacky. No need to worry. We'll have a blast and get you the answers you need. Oh, I nearly forgot. We must go this Saturday and be there at twelve noon. Is that okay?" He perks up instantly.

"That is perfect, gives me a day to prepare."

They discuss the arrangements and Charli insists on coming over to collect Blackthorn from his apartment in her Range Rover. "We can't turn up at a country estate in a clapped-out Fiat," she judges. Blackthorn agrees. Moments after she's rung off, he adds a note to the end of the interim report.

I am pleased to communicate cautionary optimism in this case and confirm that arrangements to gain access into Belwain Manor have been successful. Watch this space.

Friday morning hastens in the start of a heat wave. With temperatures way above the norm, Blackthorn spends much of the day inside, catching up with items from his to-do list. He calls Messrs. Allday, Crabham, Wallenhurst and Bentham in Marylebone, London and speaks directly with Reginald Smith. A verbal interim report is satisfactory for their purposes, according to Smith. He appears to be suitably impressed and Blackthorn even senses an element of surprise in Smith's tone, due to their PI having a sanctioned visit planned to see Kingsley-Albritton. When all other avenues had failed, Panther Investigations have done the business. Smith urges Blackthorn to adopt a circumspect approach to any dealings with Kingsley-Albritton, referring to him as a sly-old dog and someone who most definitely cannot be trusted one inch. Furthermore, he requests a further update no later than one week from today.

Blackthorn phones his mum. They chat about the hot weather, Dad feeling a little better and that the young couple down the street, who Blackthorn has never seen or heard of previously, are going to be having a baby in February. She asks him to fetch his notebook and dictates a recipe for a hot, spicy side dish that she calls Devil's Dip. He takes notes and promises to try it out when he gets a chance. He reassures her that he's doing well, eating enough and keeping safe and no, he's not seeing anyone special right now. He sends his love and puts the phone down guiltily as he didn't get around to mentioning Charli. However, he reassures himself that it is much too early in their relationship to be broadcasting anything. If he had mentioned her to Mum, he would surely have endured an inquest including, no doubt, when should she expect the tolling of wedding bells. At this stage, Charli just happens to be a pretty, witty, intelligent, totally amazing girl who he's only just met. Someone helping him with a case. That's it, she's just a work colleague. Omission justified.

He contemplates how events are likely to transpire tomorrow at Belwain Manor. He plans to cover all eventualities and ensures that he's perfectly prepared. He loads his Nikon SLR complete with flash mount and extra film and wonders if he needs more photography equipment. After all, he is supposed to be Charli's photographer, presumably a professional or at least, a more than competent amateur. He makes a call to Pete, who reassures him.

"Unless this guy is also a professional photographer, he won't have a clue whether you're doing it right or not, and in the unlikely event he questions anything, act European and wave your arms dismissively. We all have our own way of doing things and this just happens to be yours. Just be confident and don't put up with any bull."

Confidence again flows in abundance through Blackthorn's veins. "Thanks, Pete. You know, I mentioned about going for a drink at the end of this week. Well, can we make it next week? This case is taking up so much of my time right now." Pete sounds relieved.

"Actually, that's just perfect, Blacky. I have a rare Saturday off so I'm hoping to take Inga to the coast in the morning, probably down to Swanaby-on-Sea. This heat is oppressive for us poor Danes, you know. A cool, salty dip will be just what the doctor ordered."

Blackthorn knows that Pete has his Pete Smile switched on right now.

"Have an amazing time, my friend. Give my love to Inga and we can catch up on Monday, if you survive death by a thousand bodily pleasures, that is." They chuckle. "I should have some really important stuff for you to develop then too." Pete is, as ever, more than happy to help his friend and wishes him luck on the case before hanging up.

Blackthorn takes Wanda for a ride around town but it's brutal under the helmet, even in the last heat of the day and he decides to return home and get an early night. He has a big day ahead tomorrow. He's tempted to call Charli to not only ensure that everything is still good for the morning, but also because he just wants to hear her voice. He decides against it though after much deliberation and apartment pacing. He's confident that she's not the sort to let him down and if there was a problem, he's sure that she'd have called. As far as the voice thing, he needs to play cool, he guesses. Blackthorn is not one to push himself forward in these situations, but he can't deny the truth, he can't wait to see her. They've arranged for her to arrive outside his apartment at eleven and he'll meet her down there.

He looks around and reminds himself to buy a carpet as soon as he's got time and funds, and with that, he gets to bed, and sleep comes upon him quickly.

Chapter Thirteen

BLACKTHORN WAKES AT EIGHT and completes a morning jog around his sitting room, precisely twenty times. It takes almost two minutes and he wonders what on earth those in the apartment below must be thinking. He's sure that having no carpet must sound like a herd of elephants to them, as his dad might say. He showers and decides on making an egg sandwich for breakfast. but upon inspection, the few remaining slices of bread left in the kitchen have gone moldy. He switches on the radio and listens to the local BBC station. The heat wave is going to continue throughout the weekend but expect thunderstorms late on Monday.

He dresses for a day of being a photographer, in blue Levi jeans, a white T-shirt sporting a Guinness logo topped off with a white Nikon baseball cap. His trusty Dr. Martens complete his outfit and he takes breakfast, not for the first time, in Ronko's, a nearby sandwich shop. He buys a Breakfast Special consisting of a baguette, bacon, egg, sausage and an unusual brown sauce that he can never identify but is delicious all the same. One of these days, he intends to question Ronko about the sauce. He's a huge friendly Turkish guy with a moustache, greasy hair and a smile the width of the Bosphorus, as the handwritten sign in the window describes, but Blackthorn decides that today is not going to be that question day. He takes his time digesting the monstrous breakfast and makes his way back home, checking Wanda on his way in. "Sorry old girl," he says to her, patting her seat as he walks past. "I'm hob-knobbing it today in a Range Rover. You've got the day off."

He makes his way back up to the fourth floor and relaxes at the little table which allows full view of the car-parking area below. He places his prepared rucksack on the bare floor and readies himself for the day ahead. He can't wait to see Charli.

At five to eleven, she pulls up. The Range Rover is gleaming, even in the shadow of the apartments. Blackthorn is down the steps in a flash but strolls out casually when in sight of his model for the day. He motions to deter her from getting out and opens the passenger door, climbs in and places his rucksack on the floor next to his feet.

"Hey, Blacky, PI. Good to see you. Will I do?"

He takes in the vision next to him. "Now let me see," he replies and begins a deliberate and contrived assessment. She has curled her hair, with the right side longer than the left. A red and blue striped headband disappears under the longer side but sports a big bow on the shorter one. She's wearing a short, two-tone red, sleeveless dress with the thinnest of straps that has an embroidered trim to the plunging neckline. Beautiful bare, tanned legs sink down into black high-heeled shoes. Classy but sexy as hell, observes Blackthorn. Perfect. "Wow," he eventually gasps. "You are one gorgeous model."

She giggles and smiles "Why, thank you, kind sir." She leans across and he magnetically leans towards her. They kiss in front of the rearview mirror, and it's their longest and most passionate to date. He eventually surfaces and notices a large blue canvas bag on the back seat.

"We're only going to Little Belwain, Charli. Not away for a few days." He realizes the implications of what he's just said and gulps. Get a grip, he tells himself.

"Ha, I'm going to be a model for the day, as well as completing my thesis, of course. Don't forget the thesis, Blacky. Anyway, models always have lots of outfits to wear so I've brought a small collection. I know we've got work to do but there's no harm in having a bit of fun at the same time, is there?"

"No harm at all,' agrees Blacky. "Now Miss Charli Wentworth-Kent, let's get this show on the road. Wagons roll!"

Throughout their journey, they run through a mini rehearsal of their plan. Nothing is to be left to chance. They will be the ultimate professionals. The radio is switched on to a popular music channel and as they pass the sign for Little Belwain, Olivia Newton-John's Xanadu begins to play.

"Wowzers! If that isn't an omen, I don't know what is," declares Blackthorn, with a degree of optimism. Charli agrees in sheer bewilderment.

They make their way along the lane and note that Mike's van is parked on his drive though the Granada is not. They reach the entrance of Belwain Manor at precisely eleven fifty-five and pull in off the lane and stop in front of the gates. "I'll just be a sec,' says Charli as she slides out the car but before she can reach the entry system button, the gates begin to open.

She turns to face Blackthorn still seated inside. She shrugs her shoulders.

I guess we're expected. Welcome to Xanadu," and with that, she's back at the wheel. The Range Rover progresses slowly down the stone-crunching drive that meanders its way towards the large house beyond. As Belwain Manor comes impressively into view, they notice a familiar Ford Granada parked in the courtyard.

"Xanadu," exclaims Blackthorn, and his driver smiles. Moments later, the large front door to the house opens and Mike Twinner appears, waving his hands that way airport marshalling staff do when giving direction to pilots. He consequently points to the ground to indicate where they should park. There is no sign of Kingsley-Albritton. As the Range Rover comes to a halt, Mike is at once at Charli's driver's door, opening it for her as though royalty has arrived. He takes Charli's hand and helps her out. Of course, he does.

"Welcome to Belwain Manor," proclaims Mike proudly, as though he owns the place. Blackthorn gets out without assistance or any acknowledgement for that matter. "You look absolutely divine, dearest niece. An improvement on that Fiat, I see," he continues, in a voice louder than it need be, as though auditioning for a part in a play.

"Thank you, Uncle Mike," plays Charli. "I can't thank you and Mister…the owner here, sorry, I've forgotten his name."

"Kingsley-Albritton. Bartholomew Kingsley-Albritton at your service, my dear." They locate a frail-looking man sitting in a wheelchair in the doorway of the manor. Despite the heat of the day, he is dressed in a dark suit with a blue blanket covering his waist down to just below his knees.

His shiny black, highly-polished shoes suggest a possible military background, notes Blackthorn. Charli responds with a simple wave as she grabs her bag from the rear seat and Blackthorn, carrying his rucksack, now on his back, approaches the seated owner of Belwain Manor.

"Good to meet you, sir," he offers. "We appreciate your kind assistance on this beautiful day. What a wonderful home you have here."

He senses Kingsley-Albritton evaluating the situation but they're both instantly distracted by Charli's enchanting giggles as she walks arm-in-arm with her temporary uncle who appears, to Blackthorn at least, too friendly by half.

"You can…" he begins, staring at Charli before giving the merest of glances in the direction of Blackthorn. "You can call me Barty. It's short for Bartholomew. I was named after the famous St. Bartholomew's Hospital in the City of London where my father was a renowned surgeon." Blackthorn can hardly believe his ears. The veteran recluse is opening up to them as though they're the closest of friends. Charli extricates herself from Mike and delivers a lingering kiss on Barty's cheek.

"Well, I'm Charli Victoria Kingston and I'm delighted to meet you, Mr. Barty," she lies, seductively. Her bubbly and confident nature appears to briefly disarm their host. "I'm sure Uncle Mike has told you about the thesis I have to complete for uni but that shouldn't take long. Then, if it's okay with you, Jonathan here," she gestures towards Blackthorn, "will take some photos for my model portfolio. That is okay, isn't it?"

Barty clears his throat. "Consider that request approved, young lady. Pray, what is in such a large bag?" He's poking at the canvas bag being carried by Charli with a long-pointed finger that resembles one belonging to an ancient wizard.

"A change of tops, skirts, dresses, a couple of swimsuits—you get the idea." There is absolutely no doubt from his expression that Barty has got the idea, hook, line and sinker, but he remains seated all the same. Barty spins the wheelchair to face the interior of the grand house, and without a glance behind him, calls out an instruction.

"Thank you, Michael. You've seen your niece. You can go now. I'm sure you can catch up another time." Blackthorn detects a disappointed frown from Mike. Being unceremoniously dismissed in such fashion is demeaning, to say the least. Mike solemnly shakes Blackthorn by the hand and gives Charli a long, never-to-be seen again sort of hug.

"Now, Michael!" repeats an inflexible voice from inside the house and moments later, Mike is inside the Granada and heading up the drive.

Chapter Fourteen

BLACKTHORN LOOKS AT CHARLI in a knowing way. The feeble-looking wheel-chaired old man is certainly not one to be crossed. They hear the voice again from somewhere inside that's out of view, only this time, it's tone is now friendly, even fragile. A transformation has taken place. "I can give you two hours and no more, I'm afraid." He comes across as genuinely apologetic. "I need my sleep. This bothersome illness takes it out of me."

Blackthorn and Charli venture inside and enter a large square, flag-stoned hall, which has a high, timbered ceiling and is dominated by a substantial stone fireplace. An impressive timber staircase spirals upwards from right to left to a second floor above. They find Barty in his wheelchair next to a tall suit of armor at the far end of the hall.

"Come on in, over here," he instructs. "Don't be shy. Let's get your thesis questions out of the way, Miss Charli, so your photographer can get his work done. Time and tide waits for no man."

Charli quizzes Kingsley-Albritton with a series of questions, ranging from the history of Belwain Manor to what it's like to live in such a gloriously, impressive house. He appears relaxed and his answers natural and honest. All are documented in a notebook from Swanton University. He enlightens the two about the unfortunate tragic death of his wife in a car accident in 1974 that had led, in part, to him purchasing Belwain because he wished to live in isolation from that moment onward. The love for his deceased wife is evident and sensed by both visitors. Charli walks to the back of the wheelchair, and leans over its back, giving Barty a heartfelt hug from behind. Blackthorn thinks he notices a tear in the old man's eye but can't be certain. Charli maneuvers herself to be directly in front of Barty and drops to a squat position. Her short dress rides higher than it should. She folds back the blanket and places a hand on each of his knees.

"So, what's going on here, Barty? How come you're stuck in this thing?" His demeanor changes and he looks momentarily as if he's about to explode. "If you don't mind me asking?" continues Charli giving each knee the tiniest of squeezes.

The frail old man returns. He sighs heavily. "Multiple Sclerosis. Came on a year ago from nowhere and the damn thing is getting worse. I'm a prisoner in this chair, on this floor, in this house." His obvious agitation triggers another hug from Charli.

"I'm so sorry, Barty," she almost cries. She stands up and turns to Blackthorn.

"Okay, Jonathan. Thesis is complete. Where do you want me?" She removes her headband and lets her hair fall around her face as she shakes her head. Blackthorn and Barty catch each other's eye, and both raise their eyebrows approvingly.

The Nikon gets to work, with a little help from Blackthorn, of course. Some of the positions that Charli gets herself into suggests that she's done this before, though she's previously denied it. The first shots are taken inside the house. Charli drapes herself over pieces of period furniture, lies prostrate in front of the fireplace and poses provocatively around the newel post at the foot of the staircase, all the time scrutinized by the avid, wheel-chaired spectator.

After fifteen minutes or so, Blackthorn asks Barty for permission to continue in the grounds. Barty raises no objection but before they venture outside, Charli delves inside her bag.

"Now gentlemen, give me a moment here please," and she begins to slip out of her dress. Blackthorn turns away and spins a reluctant Barty around to face the wall. They wait patiently before again following further instructions. "I'm good," she calls. "You can look now." They gasp in unison. She completes a twirl for their approval. She's changed into a pink, one-piece swimsuit with a low front and back that leaves little to the imagination. She's retained the black, high-heeled shoes.

"Stunning, my dear," Barty splutters. "Let's get you out on that lawn," directs Blackthorn.

The model and her photographer make their way to the vast, less than perfectly manicured lawn behind the house via oversized French windows situated at the rear of the hall. "Is he watching?" enquires Blackthorn. Charli spies Barty, still wheelchair bound, sitting at the French windows and she gives him an enthusiastic wave. He offers a meager wave in return. Blackthorn begins to take more shots at more angles, more enthusiastically than ever. It occurs to him that Pete will love developing these and will want to know all the gossip about the model too.

There's a retaining wall intersecting the lawn, a few hundred feet or so from the house. Charli models on it as a professional might and Blackthorn continues to click away.

"Here goes," she says to Blackthorn. "Are you ready?" It's a hot day and he's already sweating.

"As ready as I'll ever be." She stands on the wall and turns away from the house, and slowly starts to remove the swimsuit but jumps down on the opposite side of the wall, out of view, before the deed is done. Quite the tease! Blackthorn skirts around the end of the wall and continues his photography duties. They give it five minutes. She stands up with the swimsuit pulled down over her shoulders and turns to half-face the house. She speaks quickly and excitedly, trying not to move her lips as if performing an act of ventriloquism.

"We have a Xanadu moment, Blacky. He's at the window. He's at the window. Barty's up at a top window. A very top window. I can see him as clear as day, and he can sure see me." She turns to face the manor and looking up, stretches her arms towards the sky. Blackthorn drops down to the soft grass and takes photos that would make even David Bailey proud. A couple of shots manage to incorporate upper windows of the manor which include a certain gentleman peering out.

The swimsuit is pulled back into its correct place and the two walk back towards the manor. Charli notes that Barty has departed the window. They enter via the French windows and meet a red-faced Barty in the hall, in his wheelchair. Blackthorn notes that the blanket is missing.

"One more shoot and we're done, Barty," informs Blackthorn, "but we need your special permission for this one."

"Ask away." Barty sounds intrigued.

"Well," begins Charli, "Uncle Mike mentioned that you own a Bentley and I would just love to have some shots in it, on it, all over it, actually," she giggles. Blackthorn recognizes the giggle instantly. The giggle that could tumble the Walls of Jericho.

"Absolutely no problem. It's parked over in the old stables across the courtyard. It's unlocked. If you need the keys, let me know." Charli sidles up to the wheelchair, leans over and whispers.

"There's just one more thing, Barty. These last shots are going to be with me," she pauses. "With me, naked. We'll be careful not to identify your car. I don't want my shots to embarrass you." Barty looks as hot and breathless as Blackthorn, and he hasn't even been outside, though he has been dashing up and down several flights of stairs in their absence.

"Go ahead. All fine by me," he recovers. Charli leans further forward, barely staying inside the swimsuit, and not for the first time, delivers Barty a kiss, this time on the lips. Blackthorn looks on with mixed emotions but recognizes that the plan is going perfectly well. Charli comes up for air, shakes her body and struts off confidently towards and through the front door. Blackthorn gives Barty a wide smile and raised eyebrows before collecting her bag of clothing and his own rucksack. He follows her outside.

The loose stones on the drive are tricky to negotiate for Charli and she removes her shoes but finds being barefooted not an enthralling prospect either.

"Jonathan," she calls tenderly, recalling the script. Blackthorn receives the message loud and clear. He straps the rucksack to his back and hands her the canvas bag of clothes. He picks her up, cradles her like a baby in his arms and carries her across to the old stables. They both enjoy the short walk. The warmth of her skin in his hands delights his senses and she relishes the comfort of his arms. She feels safe, though partially suffocated by the bag. Despite this, she allows her head to nestle into his chest. The walk lasts barely forty-five seconds. They both wish it had taken longer. He sets her down and pulls at the timber doors that creak open and the Bentley is revealed. It's a Cornich Convertible, red in color with a tan-colored hood and matching leather interior. "She's a beauty," drawls Blackthorn.

"So, you've gone off me now, have you," giggles Charli. "See a Bentley and I'm history, I guess."

"Never," replies Blackthorn, realizing that perhaps he's responded a little too quickly. He takes her clothing bag and nestles it in a corner next to his rucksack. He swings open both stable doors as wide as they will go and in his peripheral vision, catches Barty peering through a ground floor open window directly opposite.

Charli leans against the front of the Bentley, with bare feet balancing upon glistening chrome. She arches across its bodywork and Blackthorn takes photos from every conceivable angle. She knows Barty is watching, so she slides off the car and makes a move as if to begin peeling off the swimsuit. She wanders a few paces to her right and disappears out of sight from the voyeur at the Manor.

Blackthorn is remaining professional, although he can't help but be dazzled by the figure before him. "How am I doing?" Charli asks, as if to be reassured.

"You're simply wonderful. I mean, you're okay, I guess." She smiles and omits the tiniest of giggles this time.

"Naked we said, didn't we?" she teases.

"Don't you dare," replies Blackthorn who catches his breath mock-fashion and hurriedly places his eye into the camera lens as though that won't count as looking. He steps backwards into position and stops in direct view of Barty. He takes a few more photos, then gives quiet instructions. "This is it, Charli. Do your worst!"

Her hand searches inside Blackthorn's rucksack. A minute later, she omits an agonizing scream that Blackthorn fears will raise the dead. Perfect! He turns and runs through the open doors, arms waving frantically with shouting that borders upon hysteria.

"Help! Help! There's been an accident!" It takes mere seconds for the front door to burst open and out sprints an athletic Barty, doing a wonderful impression of someone training for an Olympic event, albeit for more elderly gentlemen. As quick as you like, Blackthorn disappears back inside the Old Stables and snaps away from the side of the door at the rapidly advancing Bartholomew Rupert Kingsley-Albritton.

"Gotcha!" he whispers.

"What's happened?" calls an out-of-breath Barty. "Is Charli alright?" He pushes past Blackthorn before waiting for an answer. Blackthorn is surprised by the strength of the wiry old man who dashes into the building and immediately notices Charli lying face down on the cobblestone floor, a few feet from the Bentley. She is a sight to behold, particularly when feigning injury in that swimsuit, observes Blackthorn. Barty stoops down beside her, crying out her name.

"Charli! Charli!" Barty is distraught and relieved to discern some movement. She sounds dazed.

"Uncle Mike, is that you?" she asks groggily without turning her head.

"It's Barty, Barty Kingsley-Albritton, my dear," he declares. He holds her shoulder and begins to roll her over. She lets out a yelp of pain. "Can you move at all?" he asks, maintaining a high level of concern.

"I think so, maybe a little," she whimpers, and moments later, she's getting to her feet, aided by Barty on one side and Blackthorn on the other. Barty cannot help but notice that she appears to have cut her head. Blood is in her hair and running down her right temple.

"I'll call an ambulance," continues Barty. Blackthorn seizes the opportunity. "Will you take her, Barty? Please. An ambulance will take forever out here."

"Sure, I can. Yes. I mean, no, I can't possibly, my illness," he conveniently recalls and stops himself from elaborating further. "Well, I can't take her. I'm not insured," adds Blackthorn.

"Oh, Barty, you're standing, you can walk," announces Charli, pointing to his legs. "That's great news." Barty appears outraged by the scrutiny and metamorphoses from helpfully sympathetic to monster.

"You won't understand, nor should I expect you to. It comes and goes."

"Comes and goes," Blackthorn blurts out disbelieving every word. "Barty, c'mon. You were sprinting across the stones a moment ago like Allan Wells!" Barty looks ashamed for just an instant but quickly regains his composure with an indignant frown. His demeanor is now a mirror of that which earlier dismissed Mike.

"I believe your time is up. It's time for you both to leave. Now!"

He marches away back towards the front door, as perfectly straight as a soldier on parade, without a hint of disability. The front door is slammed unceremoniously shut. Blackthorn had seconds earlier busily added to his collection of incriminating Barty photos while Charli wipes away the fake movie blood with a hand towel and slips on a white T-shirt and brown, leather mini-skirt, all gathered from her clothes bag.

"Mission accomplished, Charli," announces Blackthorn with a certain degree of pride. "Now it's time we were out of here. I do believe we've outstayed our welcome." She holds his face and gently kisses his cheek. They begin the stroll back to the Range Rover and Charli interlocks her arm with Blackthorn's and complete the short walk arm in arm. Both the canvas bag and rucksack are deposited on the rear seats and the couple head off back in the direction of Swinborough. They were never to set eyes on Bartholomew Rupert Kingsley-Albritton or Belwain Manor ever again.

Chapter Fifteen

A FEW DAYS LATER, Blackthorn travels to the village of Kingsley Pease on Wanda where he meets up with George McPullis at his house. George has managed to ensconce himself into a large, old armchair in his sitting room and is being waited on hand and foot by Mary, his ever-doting wife of forty-six years.

"Thank goodness he's agreed to get out of that bed at last," rejoices Mary to Blackthorn. "Another few days of going up and down those stairs may just have finished me off for good." She's smiling, and George is within earshot.

He retorts, "Aye, and then I'd have starved to death but at least we'd have gone together. I'm never leaving you, you know."

"Cut it out, you two," intervenes their visitor in jest. "I've ridden all the way here to get business done, not to see you two canoodling."

George and Mary both laugh out loud. "There's always time for a wee bit of canoodling, my boy. You make sure you remember that, for all time," George instructs wisely. Mary agrees to go make some tea while George beckons Blackthorn over to the armchair. The young PI pulls out a large envelope from his rucksack and hands it over.

George thumbs through the many photographs, developed by Pete Briggenssen the night before. He next scrutinizes the typed report. "Conclusive, wouldn't you say?" suggests Blackthorn, but George looks far from convinced. He has a heavily furrowed brow and displays a concerned look across his well-worn features. He twists his lips in an anxious manner and for the third or fourth time, Blackthorn is losing count, silently shuffles through the layers of photos. The suspense and silence are killing Blackthorn.

"What on earth have I done wrong?" he eventually asks.

"What have you done wrong? Isn't it obvious to you?" George sounds stern and maintains his close examination of the paperwork on his lap. "Panther! Where do I start?" Blackthorn turns away and walks slowly towards the window at the far end of the room. He can feel his face redden and he gulps deeply. He reaches the window, parts the net curtains and peers out. There's a small lawn with borders of bright flowers and a meticulously trimmed hedge hiding the street beyond, but he's unable to stay focused on any of it.

"This is what is wrong with it," announces George, breaking the awkward silence at last. "Absolutely nothing! It's a fine piece of detective work. I love it and truth be known, I could only have done a wee bit better myself." His face is a picture, full of wrinkles and a grin from ear to ear. Blackthorn places his hand on his chin and shakes his head. "You rascal, you bloody old rascal."

He's pointing at George, finger wagging. "You had me going there, for a second or two anyway."

Mary reappears carrying an Oxo motif tray with a small white porcelain teapot with matching milk jug, sugar bowl, three cups and saucers and teaspoons.

"Perfect timing, Gorgeous, but we should be breaking out some bubbly. This young man has cracked this case, this difficult case, with tact and an expertise that not too many would match. I chose you, Panther, because I liked you from the first time we met up in Birmingham. Do you remember?"

"Of course. I'll never forget it." George continues. "I know this case was on your patch, but I could have given it to anyone, all with years more experience than yourself. I'm happy to say, to declare here and now, that you didn't let me down. You've done me proud and you've done yourself proud. Thank you."

The two men shake hands with genuine friendship and admiration. George's speech conjures up a tear in Blackthorn's eye, but he manages to suppress it—just.

"Well, Handsome, tea will have to do," intervenes Mary. "Champagne must wait for another day." George reassures his wife lightheartedly. "Then tea it is. I don't much care for Champagne anyway."

With the full report submitted and a certain London law firm expressing delight in the findings, Blackthorn finds himself listening to several messages that Ellen has accumulated. There are five to be exact. The first two are both from Rob. This latest case has somehow eaten into Blackthorn's social calendar and he feels a tad guilty that he's been neglecting his friend. The next message is from another reason for said neglect. It's from Charli. He had waved her off from outside his apartment once they'd returned from Belwain Manor. She had wanted to be home when her parents returned from London and told Blackthorn she would call him the following day.

To say he was disappointed when the call never materialized is an understatement. A couple more days had passed and still nothing. Of course, he had been tempted to call her, but he was never one to push a relationship. He was certain that she would call when she was good and ready, and apparently, that time had now arrived. Her voice sounds sad from the off.

"Hi Blacky. I know you know it's me, and I'm so sorry I didn't call when I said I would. Please don't be mad. It's been a bit crazy, you see. I'm calling you from Paris. My parents arranged a last-minute trip and we left that same night as I got home from seeing you. I wanted to call you so badly. We're here for a couple of days and then heading for the Cote d'Azur. Then it's Rome, Venice and somewhere else. I can hardly keep up. Truth is after that, I'm going to go on my world trip. It's something I've promised myself. I've had such a blast with you, truly I have, and maybe after all this is over…" Ellen decides to cut her off. Blackthorn ends listening to anymore messages. The final two can wait.

He saunters over to the bare sitting room window and gazes out aimlessly. He contemplates how her message was going to end. "…and maybe after all this is over, we'll get a proper chance to say our goodbyes."

"We can hook up again, get engaged, married and have kids together."

"We'll have gone our separate ways, so to part now is probably for the best." The options seem endless. What is certain is that Charli, the most beautiful and fun-loving girl he's ever met, who genuinely seemed to like him, has gone, possibly forever.

He reminisces about the night of their meeting at Miss Ritzy's, the crazy wolf outfit that lead him to Charli, their adventures out in Little Belwain and how together, they had cracked the impossible case of Kingsley-Albritton. How the old man of Xanadu had fallen head over heels in a matter of minutes with this vision of beauty, which had proved instrumental in his downfall. Blackthorn surmises that Kingsley-Albritton and himself may have more in common with each other than he could ever have imagined.

He is about to call Rob but stops as the two red numbers now gleaming away on Ellen catch his eye. Is one of the final two messages from Charli, calling back to finish off her previous call? Blackthorn decides not to take any chance and sets Ellen back into action.

The first is from a local solicitor firm requesting that Panther Investigations act as its process server. This usually entails delivering court documents to individuals, often without that person's approval. In Blackthorn's limited experience, process serving falls into two categories, distinctly mundane and downright dangerous. He knows the solicitors well and will get back to them tomorrow.

He crosses his fingers as the last message begins. He is hoping to hear Charli's voice. He doesn't. It's some guy called Jerome Thomas from Ladywear InterContinental, a large factory employer in Swinborough. He's explaining that they have a security problem that they need to discuss with the proprietor of Panther Investigations. Mr. Thomas stresses that the call has been made following a referral from a mutual friend. He requests a call back as soon as possible. Blackthorn is intrigued but remains disappointed that it wasn't Charli. He shakes himself down and decides to ring Rob. Process serving and problems at Ladywear InterContinental can wait for now. What he really needs is a pint or two to take his mind off Charli.

Chapter Sixteen

B LACKTHORN IS IN THE OFFICES of Symmonds, Arnold & Scottman. He's aware that Rita, who is sitting behind a tall reception desk, is flirting with him—again. Her task in hand is to pass over the large envelope containing papers which he will duly serve, following the instructions contained therein. This time is no different from all other visits, at least when Rita is manning the front desk. She will be fifty-something, and one of those jovial souls who never appears less than thrilled to be alive. She stands up to hand over the envelope but as Blackthorn reaches out, she snatches it away and chuckles, as she does on every occasion. He knows what's coming next, and while it's all predictable, it's sort of endearing in a peculiar way.

"If I were thirty years younger, Blackthorn, you wouldn't know what had hit you." Rita is a little on the buxom side and each time she says these things,

Blackthorn puts on a brave face, and adds a smile that James Bond might be proud of when conversing with Miss Moneypenny. "C'mon Rita. I'm in a hurry today. I've got so much on right now."

She leans forward against the tall counter with the envelope held at a safe distance against her right shoulder. "You can always come and get it." A nearby office door opens, and Blackthorn is saved. Into the reception area strides one of the partners, Allen Scottman. Rita quickly thrusts the envelope in Blackthorn's direction and sits back down in the blink of an eye. He gratefully accepts.

"Everything okay here?" enquires the solicitor.

"Everything is under control," announces Blackthorn. "I'm on my way out," and turns to leave. "Before you go," adds Mr. Scottman, "You'll be serving those papers on old Len Battesford down at Crickworth Farm. Just a word of warning, Mr. Panther. He's not an easy character to find and even more difficult to get along with. Oh, I believe the instructions mention geese. Be aware of the geese. Be very aware of the geese. I speak from personal experience."

Blackthorn is thankful for the regular work he receives from Scottman and his colleagues, and for the advice given, but seizes on the opportunity. "I'm sure you'll understand," he starts with conviction, "that any untoward experience with this serving may be reflected in my invoice."

Scottman stiffens. "We have a flat fee agreement for such work," but before he continues, he notices Blackthorn's eyebrows raise and the envelope on its way back to Rita.

"We'll see, Mr. Panther. We'll see. We may be able to display a little flexibility in this case. Just get it served and report back."

Blackthorn knows he's negotiated that one well enough and figuratively slaps himself on the back. Scottman returns to his office. Before Blackthorn exits the door, he hears Rita giving him a slow, deliberate hand clap, and then he is gone, on his way to Crickworth Farm, wherever that might be.

He's left Wanda next to a black wooden bench just down the street and that's where he sits to mull over the contents of the envelope. He learns that Crickworth Farm is located within the parish of Blunsford which he can reach in about thirty minutes. He checks his watch. It's ten past ten. He intends to get this wrapped up quickly, grab some lunch in town and then call Lady-wear InterContinental. He prefers having his days planned out in advance. He continues reading the instructions. The piece about the geese is impossible to miss. It's scribbled in red pen as an afterthought, probably by Scottman himself, Blackthorn surmises.

Beware of the Geese! They Attack!

Blackthorn has had a few run-ins with dogs in his short time as a private investigator, but geese, not so much. His only knowledge of a goose is that it's a bird, and an alternative dish at Christmas to turkey, as referred to in *A Christmas Carol* by Charles Dickens. There is also a photograph of Len Battesford with a scribbled pencil note added on the reverse. It reads, *Battesford of Blunsford*. He's unsure whether it is an attempt at humor or just an unintentional faux pas but either way, he can't help but find it amusing. He returns to the photograph. There is no doubting that Len Battesford looks a grumpy bugger. Blackthorn visualizes the image in his head, packs away the papers and tucks the envelope inside his jacket. He's soon away out of town and can almost taste the pork pie with English Mustard he's going to be having for lunch.

The heat wave has been over for a few days and recent heavy downpours have left country lanes puddled. As he makes his way deep into the rural wilderness, the road surface becomes increasingly treacherous, made more so by the amount of mud he's trying to avoid. "Worse than Little Belwain," he grumbles. He passes several farms but none of them have any signage indicating that he's arrived at the right one. The instructions were imprecise, which he finds frustrating.

He takes Wanda further along the lane than he feels is necessary and turns her around. He slows at the first farm alongside a large corrugated-iron barn.

He can hear a tractor engine close by and stops at an open gateway. He dares not take Wanda further in as the mud is way too deep and most definitely of a questionable nature. He looks for an identification sign but there isn't one. He wonders how successful deliveries of any kind fair out here. While he's wondering, he fails to detect a brawny farmhand approaching from his left. He gets a tap, or more accurately, more of a light thump on his shoulder and is confronted by a red face doing a lot of talking. He thinks this man is speaking English, but he can barely understand a word. He decides to respond with slow talk as if addressing a foreigner.

"I am looking for Crickworth Farm, Mr. Battesford. Do you know where that is?"

He receives a few words that he's unable to catch, but a massive finger points directly at a cluster of buildings a little way down the lane on the opposite side, perched atop a small hill. As Blackthorn begins to move Wanda forward, more words are imparted in his direction, only with increased intensity and animation. He may be becoming a little paranoid, but he swears he hears the geese word again. "The only word I can understand and it's 'geese.'"

He steels himself. He is not going to allow a few daft birds to come between him and serving papers on Len Battesford. He waves his thanks to the man standing in several inches of muck and shortly afterward, he's at the end of a long muddy track that slopes uphill to a red brick farmhouse that's surrounded by a variety of barns and other outbuildings. He notices a very old, rotting wood sign partially overgrown that confirms his arrival at Crickworth Farm. It's lying at an angle and the white paint is barely legible.

He's forced to occasionally step Wanda up the track in areas where the mud deepens. He guesses that the recent heat wave may have entirely missed the parish of Blunsford. Wanda comes to a halt in front of a narrow, gated path that leads up to the front door of the farmhouse. In case a quick getaway is required, Blackthorn maneuvers Wanda to face the direction from whence she came and leaves the ignition key in place. Must be ready for any eventuality.

He removes his crash helmet and listens intently. All is quiet and thankfully, not a single goose to behold. There's an old maroon-colored Thames Pick-Up parked in the entrance to a nearby barn.

While rather decrepit, Blackthorn concludes it's probably operational as it's displaying a current tax disc. Not so the yellow Morris Drop-Side Truck abandoned at the side of a brick, low-roofed outbuilding that has most definitely given up the ghost. The truck doors are wide open, and part of a tree is growing out from where the windscreen used to be. The tyres have disintegrated and rust is running riot over the metalwork.

Blackthorn turns his attention to the farmhouse itself. There are discolored net curtains at the windows and both window frames and front door are in desperate need of a lick of paint. He momentarily considers that the entire place could be deserted. "Anybody here?" he calls, without much conviction, it should be said. There is no response. Semi-derelict and deserted. Is he about to discover the body of Len Battesford, long since deceased?

Armed with the court summons, he pushes open the crooked, low gate that drags on the rough paving beneath. The area between gate and farmhouse front door that was once a lawn is now enveloped in a multitude of thistles and other weeds. There is no doorbell, but he does locate a brass, green-tarnished door knocker in the shape of a ram's head. A horseshoe hangs precariously on a single crooked nail tapped into the low timber beam above.

Blackthorn takes a deep breath and bangs the door with the ram's head. He can discern an echo inside as though the old place is empty. He repeats the action a few moments later and still, there's no reply. He moves stealthily across the frontage, taking care where each step lands, and peers through one of the windows. It is filthy, and he spits on his hand to wipe a small clearing on the glass. He can barely make out a thing at first but as his eyes adjust, he glimpses items of furniture, a large dining table and a few scattered chairs. He's attempting to make out more when he's startled from above.

"What you up to?" booms out a voice. He follows the voice and sees Len Battesford leaning out of an upstairs window, directly above his head. "Mr. Len Battesford, I presume," replies Blackthorn, recalling the historical meeting in Africa between Dr. David Livingstone and Henry Stanley in 1871.

"Get off my land," demands Battesford in a forceful tone. "Whatever you're selling, I'm not buying." Blackthorn moves away from the house to get a better view of Battesford and to add a degree of comfort to his neck muscles.

"I'm not selling anything, sir, but I do have something of great interest to you." Len Battesford certainly comes across as an aggressive and disagreeable individual.

"If you don't clear off, I'll set the dogs on you," he threatens. Blackthorn looks around and theatrically cups a hand to his ear. He's comforted not to hear any growls, howling or barking. He's thinking fast. Very fast.

"Sir, I've been visiting farms in the area and I understand you have geese. I don't have anything for dogs, I'm afraid, but there is an airborne goose disease that is rife throughout the county and its bringing down the poor birds in huge numbers. You must have heard of it? It's been all over the news." Blackthorn has already noted that there is no television aerial in sight and elects to take this calculated risk.

Battesford appears thoughtful, concerned and finally resigned to the inevitable. His voice settles into a more moderate tone. "How d'you know I've got geese?"

"The farmer down the way there told me," Blackthorn says, pointing across the adjacent open fields in no particular direction."

"Who told you?"

Blackthorn continues as though the question was never asked. "I must tell you, sir, that without treatment, you may lose your entire flock. I have been sent by County Animal Protection Services to give you an antidote to this vicious virus strain, and where there's bad news, there should also be good news. There's no worry about any cost because it's free. I truly urge you to accept, if you love your birds."

"Leave it down there on the step. I'll collect it later," groans Battesford.

"If only I could," adds Blackthorn ruefully. "You have to sign for it first, otherwise they make you pay for it. Ridiculous I know. The cost is five hundred pounds, but with your signature, there is, thankfully, no charge. That's why they've sent me and my colleagues to farms across the county to track down geese and their owners in an attempt to stop this terrible disease in its tracks. God-forsaken job if you ask me, but I guess someone must do it to save these poor birds. I trust I can rely on you to do the right thing, sir. You do have geese, don't you?"

"You must know I do. I'll be down," and with that, he disappears from the window which he leaves open. Blackthorn side steps across to the front door and waits.

A minute or so passes before Blackthorn becomes aware of heavy footsteps from inside the house, getting louder as they approach until they stop on the other side of the front door. It opens slowly with a long, rusty creak that would make a great sound effect for a horror movie. The door scrapes the uneven, paved floor, and there he is, Mr. Len Battesford, himself.

Blackthorn realizes immediately that the description given has failed spectacularly to indicate one key point and the photograph in his possession has also failed to do the man confronting him any justice. Len Battesford is a giant of a man. His enormous build fills the entire door frame but to his credit, Blackthorn stands his ground.

"Where's this here antidote stuff, then?" enquires Battesford.

"Mr. Len Battesford," begins Blackthorn and from behind his back produces a large envelope.

"Yes, yes. Get on with it, lad. I don't have all day. Where do I sign?"

Blackthorn removes the court summons from the envelope and passes it into the colossal outstretched hand before him.

"By order of the court, you are hereby duly served this summons."

What happens next, shocks the irrepressible process server. He expects Battesford to at least growl like a bear or become outraged and threaten some degree of physical violence, but no. The huge man begins to smile. Smile becomes a smirk and then smirk turns to laughter. Blackthorn retreats a few feet to better take in the scene. He can hardly believe his eyes, or ears for that matter. "Well, well. You got me. You well and truly got me. Well done. You're the best one yet. I never suspected you. Not in a million years would I have suspected you. Now if you don't mind, I have a small surprise for you."

Blackthorn is wary and looks around. His senses are on high alert. Battesford reassures him. "Don't worry lad. I'm not going to shoot you, even though I have a shotgun or two."

"It's not the dogs, is it?" questions Blackthorn. The door remains open and Battesford fades into the gloomy interior.

"I don't have dogs," he shouts back. "I'll be about a minute. Just you wait there." Blackthorn has absolutely no intention of just waiting there while Battesford disappears to go fetch he knows not what. He takes long strides to reach Wanda, and wastes no time putting on his crash helmet, but before he can start her up, he hears an odd noise. His view is restricted within the helmet, but he suddenly catches movement in his left rear-view mirror. He spies Len Battesford and he's herding the infamous geese from around the far side of the farmhouse and straight towards motorcycle and rider.

Blackthorn looks over his left shoulder. Battesford is brandishing a large staff in his hand and emitting a monstrous noise as though leading a cavalry charge, and then there's the geese, manically-driven forward. Blackthorn has no idea how many there are of them and he has no intention of hanging around to conduct a geese audit. It's safe to assume there are at least a couple of dozen, muddy white with a mix of dangerous orange and red bills to the fore, honking and hissing for all they're worth.

They appear more than agitated and it's a cacophony of geese sound that's almost upon him. He fires up Wanda and is relieved that, yet again, she doesn't let him down. He feels bites to his jeans as Wanda slips and slides through the mud, but she quickly pulls him away to safety. As he departs the farmyard, with Battesford and geese in his wake, he joyously pulls out the envelope from inside his jacket and waves it victoriously aloft. He knows there and then that he'll never be able to attempt another serving at Crickworth Farm. That thought suits him just fine.

Chapter Seventeen

H E RETURNS TO THE SOLICITORS' OFFICE, swears an affidavit with Peter Arnold, one of the partners, who is suitably impressed that Blackthorn has managed to return successful and relatively unscathed, apart from sporting a new attire of dried mud. Peter promises to pass a note on to Allen Scottman. It reads, *Thanks for mentioning the geese. No thanks for not mentioning Len Battesford is the size of Goliath. That will be an additional five pounds please. Thank you.*

Mercifully, Blackthorn manages to avoid Rita who is out to lunch, and within the hour, has satisfied his penchant for pork pie at The Lamb Inn, located just around the corner. Blackthorn returns home, gets showered and changed and is soon ready to make the telephone call to Ladywear InterContinental. The receptionist answers immediately, introducing herself as Natalie and apparently is proud to be representing Ladywear InterContinental.

"Good for you," replies Blackthorn. "I've been left a message to call Mr. Thomas."

"And which Mr. Thomas might that be?" answers Natalie.

"The Jerome version, please. Just how many Mr. Thomas's do you have?" There's a slight pause as though Natalie is either counting on her fingers or reaching for a calculator. Natalie titters down the line.

"We have three, sir. To whom do I have the pleasure of speaking?" Blackthorn is impressed by her annunciation skills.

"Let him know that Mr. Panther is returning his message," he adds, in his poshest accent. Moments later, he's connected.

"Now Mr. Panther. Please understand from the off that this is a confidential matter, and no member of my staff can know anything about it. Do you understand?"

"What's the problem, Mr. Thomas? Just come to the point if you don't mind. Everything at Panther Investigations is treated with the utmost confidence, and I guess you already know we're the best. That's why you called us." There is no doubting that, since the successful outcome of the Kingsley-Albritton case, Blackthorn's level of confidence has skyrocketed.

"Our last four stocktakes have shown deficits in inventory, with the last one just a few days ago indicating that this is a problem that's on the increase."

"Jerome—may I call you Jerome—someone is stealing from you, right?"

"Right, left and centre," he declares. "We thought we could solve it ourselves but even our in-house security team has drawn a blank."

"How much is going missing, Jerome?"

"Rather a lot, I'm afraid. We do have one lead for you though. It's definitely happening on the late shift."

Blackthorn learns that there are two shifts working the factory. The first begins at six in the morning, and they're replaced by the second shift at two in the afternoon who work through to ten at night, when the entire factory closes. Following the first theft, discovered a couple of months back, Jerome and his management team had introduced several measures to monitor the comings and goings and inventory numbers much closer than had previously been the case. The initial discovery had come about by chance rather than judgement.

Six large boxes of expensive silk underwear destined for a fashion show in Italy had simply vanished into thin air the night before their planned pick-up. Jerome had been personally involved with this order and was shocked to learn of the mysterious disappearance. An urgent overtime run to replace the missing garments had cost the company significantly but had the obvious effect of benefiting the workforce.

Since then, a multitude of products have gone missing and management were at a loss as to what to do next.

A board meeting between Jerome and his brother, Jonathan plus two senior managers, had reluctantly concluded that a new face, an investigator, was needed to flush out the culprit or culprits. Their current efforts, including those of their own security team, had failed miserably. The third brother, Joshua, was as usual, absent from such meetings. Joshua is always absent. No one talks much about him other than he has issues.

Blackthorn negotiates a ridiculously high fee and tells Jerome that he will call in to see him as Mr. Smith, tomorrow morning at eleven. He puts the phone down and begins scribbling furiously into his tiny notebook. An hour passes, and he has the beginnings of a plan, but before anything else, he makes his way downstairs to poor Wanda. She's encrusted in mud from their exploits out at Crickworth Farm. He lovingly restores her to her shiny best, albeit not before darkness descends.

Next morning, Blackthorn is the first customer of the day at Party Costumes for All. The early shift girl recognizes him immediately. "Will it be one wolf costume, sir?" she jests.

"An elephant, please," states Blackthorn seriously. "It must have huge ears, a long tail and complete with a howdah."

The girl looks puzzled, even shocked. She eventually utters a response. "I don't think we have one of those," she replies meekly.

"Ah well, not to worry. Perhaps a small disguise will suffice instead. Do you have any makeup?"

Forty-five minutes later, Blackthorn is seated in the rear of a taxi on his way to Ladywear InterContinental, looking more like Hercule Poirot than Hercule Poirot. He is wearing a light blue suit, polished black dress shoes, white stiff-collared shirt, blue bow tie and a black bowler hat. His first preference of a Homberg hat was unavailable. He sports a black moustache upturned at the ends and some Skin-Work as the shop girl had called it, to add about forty years to his look. He catches sight of his own image in the rearview mirror of the taxi. He convinces himself that Agatha Christie would be proud of his creation. The taxi driver is constantly distracted by his odd-looking passenger and fortunately fails to run down several pedestrians during the short but perilous journey.

Hercule Panther enters the premises of Ladywear InterContinental through a large, brass revolving door more in keeping, he thinks, with a big city department store. For a company specializing in such tantalizing, fun and seductive products, the entrance lobby is rather austere. He thinks it odd that there's not a hint of underwear to be seen anywhere. Three large picture frames housing portraits of, presumably, the three brothers who own the company, dominate the room. He approaches a young lady sitting at a polished, period reception desk. She looks up from a typewriter and begins, "Hello, I'm..."

The visitor stops her in her tracks by raising his hand and squinting as though in deep thought. "You are." He closes his eyes and places a finger on his brow which he begins to tap. "You have something in common with Christmas. Don't tell me! Let me think. Your name is..." He pauses dramatically. "Your name is, Natalie." The receptionist looks astounded.

"That is seriously amazing, sir. My colleague, who is off sick today, is called Natalie. What a coincidence! Anyway, I'm Samantha. Please sign in on the visitor sheet." A deflated Blackthorn does as he's asked and waits in an uncomfortable chair in a gloomy corner.

"I see you're here to see Mr. Jerome. He is expecting you and shouldn't be too long, Mr. Smith." Samantha is obviously intrigued by the strangely-dressed visitor and gets little else done apart from constantly gawking at him until Jerome Thomas eventually appears.

Blackthorn is led down a dimly-lit corridor and into an office that resembles something out of a period drama. He can almost envisage Winston Churchill sitting behind the substantial desk. "May I presume," begins Jerome, "that you are in disguise, and if so, why?"

Blackthorn, for the first time, removes the bowler hat and places it on the desk in front of him. "Jerome, no-one must know my true identity here. The best way to solve this case is to go undercover. Tell me about the late shift staff. I need to know everyone who is on the premises from when the regular office staff go home to when the place closes."

Over the course of the next hour, Blackthorn becomes versed in everything he needs to know about the running of the factory and specifically, who is supposed to be where and when during the late evening shift. There are one hundred and twenty-four female employees who work the main factory floor, including supervisors and two managers. There are an additional three canteen staff finishing at eight o'clock.

Office cleaners from an outside contractor arrive at seven thirty and are expected to leave between nine thirty and ten. The main entry and exit doors are locked at six by the in-house security team who begin their own shift at five thirty. They also let the cleaners in and out. He learns there are only two security guards and despite their best efforts, whatever they are, have been unsuccessful in bringing the thieves to justice. The factory workers complete their shift at ten o'clock and all must have left the premises by ten thirty. The two security guards conduct a final inspection and lock up around eleven.

Blackthorn has scribbled incessantly into his notebook throughout the meeting, rarely looking up at Jerome Thomas. Even when Jerome has answered all the questions asked of him, Blackthorn continues to write for a further five minutes.

"I'm a terrible host," declares Jerome, breaking the silence. "Would you perhaps like a drink, Mr. Panther?" Blackthorn downs his pen.

"No drink, thank you, but I do need you to approve something."

"Go on." Jerome is leaning forward in that way people do when the suspense is killing them. "You are going to employ me as an additional security guard. Your current security duo need help. It is an obvious and inconspicuous move by management to increase security levels at such a time. I will begin in two days. Is there a problem with getting me uniformed in that time?" Jerome displays the faintest of smiles.

"Great idea and, no problem at all. We have a couple of lockers full of the stuff. I'm certain they'll be something to fit you. Come this way."

Forty minutes later, after arranging a return taxi ride through the efficient Samantha, Blackthorn is on his way home with a large polythene bag containing a rather unimpressive security uniform.

He gets dropped off at Party Costumes for All where he returns the Inspector Poirot outfit and changes back into his own clothes that have been conveniently stored for him. He finds himself having to explain to the shop girl, however, that the uniform in the bag is not for a party and he hasn't gone elsewhere for a costume. Only once he has finally allayed her doubts over giving his costume business to someone else, does she move away from the door where she had been barring his exit.

Chapter Eighteen

IT'S BEEN A WHILE SINCE BLACKTHORN has been in uniform. He's dressed in a basic navy-blue suit with Security emblazoned on each shoulder. There is also a matching peaked cap. The entire outfit feels cheap compared to the hard-wearing police uniform he once wore with pride and indeed, it would not be out of place on a rack at the costume shop. He wears a white shirt and black clip-on tie with highly polished black shoes. He's ready to find out just what is going on during the late shift at Ladywear Inter-Continental. It's a warm and dry late afternoon and as the forecast suggests more of the same, he takes Wanda on the short journey across town.

He arrives at five forty and meets with his two security colleagues in a designated office at the end of a long, narrow corridor. They don't appear pleased to see him. They stand together, whispering and give

Blackthorn the merest of nonchalant glances before continuing their secret chat.

"So, which one of you is Bill and which one's Stan?"

They turn slowly to face the new recruit who they look up and down with distain, as though a nasty smell has just entered the room. "How come you don't know?" grunts the burly one. "I thought we were getting a mastermind to help solve the sins of others."

"We don't need another guard," adds the tall, skinny one. "We're doing just fine."

Blackthorn takes the six strides necessary to cross the small office and grabs hold of the tall skinny one's hand before he can resist and shakes it. "I'm Gary Smith, and I've been told that you two are doing a great job. Straight from Mr. Thomas, Jerome Thomas that is. He believes that another pair of eyes might help get to the bottom of what's going on."

"There's nothing going on," says the tall, skinny one who breaks off the handshake indignantly."

"Look, Bill." Blackthorn is staring straight into the eyes of the tall, skinny one. "There's stuff being stolen, and we need to find out who's doing it."

"How d'you know I'm Bill?"

"Didn't I tell you? I'm Gary Smith, The Psychic."

Blackthorn is pleased that he asked for descriptions during his meeting with Jerome. The two security guards briefly look at each other before returning their attention to the whippersnapper calling himself Gary Smith. Stan, the burly one, offers advice. "It's just a few bras and knickers. The girls here don't get paid much so some of them will be helping themselves. It's hardly the crime of the century is it? And don't start me on what's right and wrong. If you ask me, they probably deserve a bit extra on top of their crappy wages. I have plenty of sympathy for them."

Bill nods his approval. They stare down Gary, awaiting a response.

"You know you're right. This company will be making thousands, if not millions, and a few things going missing here and there is nothing in the whole scheme of things. Barely worth bothering about. Am I right?" The atmosphere changes in an instant. Bill reconnects with the handshake and Stan offers a reassuring grin.

"You'll do okay here, Gary," he says, nodding. "It's the girls against the management, and we're with the girls. Now c'mon. We've got work to do."

Stan barks orders military-style, even though none of them are specifically in charge. He will wait in the reception to lock up the doors after the last of the awfully mean management leave. Bill will make his way through the offices, ensuring that all windows are secured, and staff have left. Officer Gary Smith is instructed to patrol the factory where the girls are busy working.

Blackthorn adjusts the peaked cap and swings open a set of double doors. The caldron of noise almost takes his breath away. There are large, industrial sewing machines everywhere, row upon row of them, and females as far as the eye can see. The machines echo their clattering sound within the huge factory and the chatter of more than one hundred women workers competes to drown it out.

He takes a gulp and begins his task. His walk is neither a march or an amble. He reminds himself of times gone by when he patrolled the streets as a police constable, with an air of authority and calmness. He is aware of dozens of pairs of female eyes trained upon him. He suppresses a smile and remains aloof—for now. Despite all the hollering in his direction, he is focused on a door about two hundred feet away. "Come over here, darlin'," shouts one. "Don't be daft. You're old enough to be his mum," disagrees a workmate. "Grandma, more like," shrieks another, and they burst into howls of laughter. "Give us a kiss, you can arrest me anytime."

Another holds incomplete underwear against her body and sways provocatively before him. Blackthorn reaches the door desperate for relief from the catcalls. It's locked. He turns around and is most certainly the centre of attention. He's aware that a blush has descended upon his face but decides that the best form of defense is attack. The chief heckler is a middle-aged woman, overweight with an immense hairdo. He likens her to a Mother Hen surrounded by her brood, an extremely large brood at that. He heads directly towards her.

"He's coming to give you a kiss," calls one of the brood, but their leader is now silent. She's watching him approach and appears deep in thought. He stops just a couple of feet from her. A teenager from behind her squawks, "You're new, aren't you? What's your name?"

"My name is Officer Smith," he says unwaveringly, "and I will certainly appreciate the courtesy of a degree of respect, just as I would respect you if you were security, and I the skilled worker." He is unsure how this ploy will go down but doesn't take his eyes from Mother Hen for one second. "Okay, ladies," she orders, "lay off him. Welcome to Ladywear, Officer Smith. I'm Kathy. If you need to know anything, just ask. There's not anything that happens around here that I don't know about."

"I'll bear that in mind, Kathy. Thank you, and by the way," he beams, "you do remind me of my Mum."

"One time only, I promise. Now don't flinch, Officer" and she gives him a huge, enveloping hug, much to the amusement of all around. Wolf whistles fill the air followed by rapturous applause. "Now ladies," orders Kathy. "Let Officer Smith get on with his job, and it's time to get on with ours."

Gary and Kathy exchange fleeting smiles and he gets to carry on his way, without further comment. The girls return their attention to their machines and he to patrolling the factory. It's as though he's instantly become invisible to them.

Everything appears normal for the rest of his shift. Three cleaners arrive, and he engages them in conversation. They are employed by Swinborough Industrial Cleaners and create the impression of total honesty—but don't they all, he reminds himself. They're a husband and wife team and their middle-daughter who has just turned eighteen. The couple have been working at the factory for five years and seem diligent in their cleaning which they take very seriously.

The daughter has only recently joined her parents working at Ladywear, replacing another who left to work elsewhere. Blackthorn considers whether the daughter is a realistic suspect. After all, is it simply a coincidence that from her time starting at Ladywear, items have begun to go missing? However, she doesn't come across as the dishonest sort. He observes her cleaning efforts and she's been well-drilled. She doesn't miss a speck of dust and is as professional as her parents. Still, she cannot be ruled out.

The cleaners leave in a van at nine forty and Blackthorn engages with Stan and Bill twenty minutes later. He informs them that for the final part of his shift, he will patrol outside. They happily agree. It's as though they really can't wait to have Gary Smith out of their lives, despite the brief niceties earlier. The ladies from the factory leave in droves and he watches from the shadows until all have gone. The car park is empty except for Wanda and two cars, presumably belonging to Stan and Bill. It's ten-twenty-seven.

He returns to the reception area where he meets up with Stan and Bill. They're sitting in chairs usually used by daytime visitors. Not much patrolling going on here, observes Blackthorn.

"Everything okay out there?" asks Stan.

"Have you got any suspects yet?" follows Bill.

"Yes, and Yes," is the surprise reply.

"Really," snorts Stan. Both men leave their slouched positions, sit upright and lean forward expectantly. Blackthorn changes the subject.

"If I need to buy some underwear here for my girl-friend, do you think they'll give me a good deal?"

"There's staff discounts, sure," is the throwaway line from Bill, "but tell us about the suspects."

"I'd rather not say if you don't mind. It's just a hunch right now."

"Well, we do mind," growls Stan. "We're a team here. We work together. We need to know what you're thinking. I need to know what you're thinking!"

His tone has an air of aggression about it, but Blackthorn stays calm and unmoved to the obvious annoyance of his newfound interrogators. "Back to the staff discounts. I'm hoping to buy quite a lot of stuff and I'm strapped for cash. I'm going to need an amazing deal from management, I guess. Anyway, are we done here tonight?"

Five minutes later, the three security officers are walking across the car park with the factory secured behind them. Stan is the first to drive off in a Vauxhall Viva. Blackthorn is about to put on his crash helmet when Bill appears alongside him driving a Ford Escort.

"I lock the main gate, so you go first. By the way, that hunch of yours, Gary. You know, about the suspects? Is it a psychic hunch?"

"You bet it is," and with helmet in place, Wanda and Blackthorn roar off into the night.

Chapter Nineteen

THREE DAYS OF LATE SHIFT SECURITY DUTIES pass with little incident for Blackthorn. He's enjoying his role as Officer Gary Smith and has regular banter with both his two security colleagues and the factory girls. Three of them, or possibly four, surreptitiously wink at him when he walks past. There is doubt in his mind for the correct number as he believes one to have a nervous eye twitch. His hunch hasn't been mentioned again and both Stan and Bill appear to have accepted him into the ranks. Everyone's at ease with the new security recruit.

In alliance with Mr. Jerome as he now calls him, two pallets of underwear have been left abandoned on one of the loading docks for two days. Mr. Jerome and Blackthorn are referring to them as bait. This is an area where garments have gone missing previously.

Dummy spy cameras have been installed around the factory and are in obvious view of all who care to pay a modicum of attention. Real working cameras requiring monitors are likely be included in future budgets, but for now, according to Mr. Jerome, it's down to Blackthorn to solve the crimes. He hopes that tonight, the bait of unattended stock will present an opportunity to catch the thieves red-handed.

Blackthorn positions himself in a small office within the loading bay area. He has his camera and binoculars at the ready and turns the desk light off. The glass window of the office gives him the perfect view of the pallets loaded with their prized cargo. The loading bay is lit only by a couple of dim low-voltage night lights. It's accessed from the interior by one single door direct off the factory floor and two large roller shutter doors to the outside where trucks and vans enter and exit during the day.

He slips down low into the solitary office chair to begin his surveillance. Stan and Bill are doing their usual thing in other parts of the factory and the girls are busy at their machines. The cleaners will also have arrived, though they are not required to enter the loading bay. The canteen staff will be clearing up. Blackthorn hopes his wait will be a short one.

It isn't. Almost two hours pass and he's contemplating an end to his weary vigil. As he begins to pack up his rucksack, a shaft of light appears as the door from the factory floor opens. He notices a figure silhouetted in the doorway and the door is quickly closed behind them. Moments later, the same door opens and closes again. Blackthorn tracks two figures making their way towards the pallets. He listens intently as the two whisper to each other and briefly laugh. The voices are female. They reach the bait. He can now identify them as two of the brood belonging to Mother Hen Kathy, though their names are unknown to him. He assesses his preferred course of action but before being able to implement anything, the door opens again. Kathy's voice booms into the open space. "You two. Get yourselves back in here, now!"

The two scuttle out past Kathy with heads cowered as children might when being chastised. Moments later the door is slammed shut and silence once again prevails.

Blackthorn thinks things through. Were the two girls planning on stealing items from the pallets and if so, how were they going to do it? Pallets are heavy. It's possible they could have taken a few small items but even then, how did they intend to hide them? Were they going to be leaving the factory that night wearing multiple layers of underwear? It was a possibility.

He makes his way out into the factory, leaving camera and binoculars inside his rucksack under the office desk. He quickly catches Kathy's eye. He beckons her over away from the other machinists.

"And what can I be doing for you, Officer Smith?" He emits a big sigh.

"I was in the loading bay just now, Kathy." He doesn't have time to continue.

"Stupid, stupid girls," Kathy exclaims. "Please don't report them. I know I should've noticed them leave but there's so many of us, it's difficult to keep track of everyone all the time and still get my own work done. Thank goodness I've given it up."

"Given it up?" questions Blackthorn.

"Yeah, I smoked for going on thirty years but packed it in six months or so ago. Those girls should know better. You tell them, but they take no notice. It's a habit you see. Please don't file a report."

Blackthorn nods. "They went in the loading bay for a smoke?"

"Yeah, of course. Can't wait, can they, but I've told them, do it again and they're out!" Blackthorn thanks Kathy and promises that it will be their secret. "You're the best," she adds. "I owe you one." He leaves to go find Stan and Bill.

He finds Bill standing guard at the front door with a military stance, legs one stride apart and hands held behind his back. He apparently has his mind on other matters and is oblivious to Blackthorn who passes behind him, making his way into the labyrinth of corridors that house the clerical and management offices.

He observes the husband and wife cleaners busily doing what they do and continues his search for Stan. After a minute or two, he hears some giggles coming from an office a little way ahead followed by a deep voice. Then more giggles. Don't tell me. I do not believe this!

He pushes at the partially opened door and steps inside. There's Stan, lounging behind a desk in a green leather chair, with the eighteen-year old female cleaner lying on the desk in a fashion that suggested they were perhaps more than simply good friends.

She sees Blackthorn and combines an impressive acrobatic roll and jump off the desk, performed in an instant. Her eyes are wide, like a startled rabbit caught in headlights. "Nothing, no, nothing," she stammers, picking up a duster and a can of polish. She runs out of the room, pushing past Blackthorn in the process. Stan leans back in the swivel chair and clasps his hands behind his head.

"What?" he says, staring at Blackthorn. "The girl said it. Nothing to see here, Gary."

Stan's flustered for sure and doing his best to cover it up. Blackthorn says nothing but shakes his head disapprovingly, turns and leaves. He returns the way he came, back to the entrance lobby. Along the route, he sees the girl cleaner who averts her eyes immediately from his. Her embarrassment is evident. Let that be a lesson to you, he hopes, with a faint degree of optimism.

Blackthorn's brain is working overtime. If Stan has a thing going on with the young cleaner girl, maybe the two of them are working together to steal stuff. He recalls that the thefts only began once she'd started working with her parents at the factory. What easier way might there be to have Stan, Stan The Security Man, to cover up for you, or even steal for you? The girl is a pretty little thing, and Stan probably can't believe his luck. Silly old fool. She only wants you for the free underwear. Surely it can't be for any other reason.

In the lobby, the doors are locked, and Bill is elsewhere. Blackthorn resumes his patrol and decides to go fetch his rucksack from the loading bay office. He opens the door to the loading bay and shields his eyes momentarily from the bright lights within. There's a white Ford Transit backed into the loading bay and one of the roller shutter doors is open. The rear doors of the transit are open too, and who should be sitting in the driver's seat of a forklift maneuvering a pallet of bait underwear into its rear is—Bill! With the whine of the forklift, Blackthorn's entrance goes unnoticed. He sneaks into the office and within seconds, he's snapping photos of the condemning evidence.

How could Bill be so stupid? Another figure comes into view from the far side of the van and although Blackthorn has never met the man, he recognizes him immediately. Joshua Thomas! The black sheep of the family, a co-owner of the company. The troubled soul. The brother with the issues. His large portrait in the lobby identifies him as the thief. But why is he stealing from his own company, and can that then be theft in the eyes of the law? All these thoughts go through Blackthorn's mind, but he continues to secretly snap away with his Nikon. He stays low and watches in silence as the bait cargo is loaded and Joshua Thomas drives away with his booty, giving a "thumbs up" to Bill out of the driver's window as he departs.

Bill returns the forklift to its usual parking space, lowers the roller shutter doors and turns the main lights off. He's about to exit via the door to the factory when it's flung open by Stan.

"Have you seen Gary?" puffs Stan. It's evident he's either been running or just enjoyed a session with the cleaner's daughter. "No", replies Bill, his tone indicating an amount of relief. I thought he was with you. You were supposed to be keeping an eye on him." Stan looks sheepish. "He caught me with Suzi. Then he disappeared. I've been searching the place but can't find him anywhere. Anyway, presumably Crazy Brother got his fix," Bill seems satisfied.

"He sure did, well pleased he was. A nice little earner."

He hands over a few notes to Stan, though it's impossible to see exactly how much. "All we have to do now is raise some suspicion on the girls again, or maybe Officer Gary Smith." The voice recorder laying on the floor next to the slightly open office door does its magic. "Let's go find Officer bloody Smith," snarls Stan. "Mr. Know-It-All psychic security kid might just be in too deep for his liking by the time I've finished with him." With that, the exit door is shut, and Blackthorn is alone.

He waits fifty minutes or so and carefully exits the loading bay and sneaks around the outside of the machinist area, which is now deserted. He checks his watch. It's ten forty-two. The cleaners will also have long gone. Only the three security personnel should now be on the premises. He goes to the far side of the factory and stands just inside the door to the female lavatory, marked as such, on a heavy swing door. He waits for the inevitable. He doesn't have to wait long. "Gary! Where are you?" It's Bill calling, having entered from the lobby.

"I'm here Bill," cries Blackthorn. "Just coming." They meet up and enter the lobby where Stan, Stan, The Angry Security Man, looks ready to blow a gasket.

"Where the hell have you been, Smith? We've been waiting to lock up for ages." So much for first name comradery.

"I had an idea. I would secrete myself into one of the female toilets and listen for any clues about the thefts. It's a well-known fact that toilets are a breeding ground for loose talk."

"As well as other things," laughs Bill. Stan is not so amused. "Shut up! This is no laughing matter. And what if the girls caught you? Didn't think of that, did you?"

Blackthorn produces a crumpled handwritten poster from his pocket. *OUT OF USE.*

"For the record," begins Blackthorn, "I came up a blank. Nothing to report." Stan gives a scheming look.

"I'm concerned that you went missing for quite a long time tonight. We searched everywhere for you. We only have your word for where you were. I hope nothing has gone missing. We wouldn't want to be suspecting you now, would we?" Blackthorn is happy to let him continue. "After all, you've been asking about staff discounts and how strapped for cash you are right now. Let's hope there haven't been any more thefts."

Blackthorn is dismissive. "Yes, I certainly hope so, Stan. Goodnight. I'll leave you two to lock up. I'm off." And in the blink of an eye, the PI is heading out of the factory gates on Wanda, eager to write his report and looking forward to seeing Pete in the morning to have some rather fruitful photographs developed. Tonight, though remaining a mystery in so many ways, has been another milestone success for Blackthorn Panther, PI.

Chapter Twenty

AT NINE FIFTEEN NEXT MORNING, Blackthorn is speaking on the phone with Jerome Thomas. "The bait was taken, Mr. Jerome. Did you see?"

"I certainly did. I hope we have some answers." Blackthorn revels in the moment.

"We certainly do, but I'm not too sure you're going to like what I'm going to tell you." There's a slight pause at the end of the phone, and Blackthorn can hear a deep sigh. "Do you have definite proof of what you're about to disclose, Mr. Panther?" There is not a hint of hesitation from Blackthorn.

"I do indeed, both verbal and visual. The photographs will be developed by this time tomorrow. Would you like to know who is responsible? I can tell you this minute, if you wish."

"Mr. Panther. You are very good at what you do, as my initial referral suggested."

Blackthorn interrupts. "Who exactly is your referral, if you don't mind me asking, Mr. Jerome?"

"Not at all. It was my cousin, Lewis Crabham. He's a partner of a law firm in London and you solved a case for them very recently. I thought I'd have to get some bigwig private detective from London to come solve our problem. I called Lewis for advice and a reference. It was he that suggested that you were my best bet and located right on my doorstep. I could hardly believe it, and you say that you know who's been doing the stealing?"

"Let me say this. I know who took this bait underwear. Now whether the same are guilty of taking all the other stuff, that is yet to be proved. Mr. Jerome, are you ready to learn the ugly truth?"

"Ready as I'll ever be."

Blackthorn relates the events of the previous evening, of Stan wasting the time of the cleaning girl who is thirty years or more his junior, of discovering that the bait was stolen by his own brother, Joshua, aided and abetted by Bill, with Stan's knowledge, and that their likely alibi will be that either Blackthorn himself or the factory girls had been the perpetrators. Jerome listens attentively as Blackthorn plays the damning voice recordings down the phone. Blackthorn concludes his verbal report. There's silence at the other end of the phone. "Are you still there?"

There's that sigh again.

"Joshua is a troubled soul, as I'm sure you've heard."

"I've heard rumors, though no specific details. I can find out, if you wish." Jerome refuses to take Blackthorn up on his offer.

"No need, Mr. Panther. Sadly, I know only too well of my brother's problems. He's our youngest and into drugs and gambling. Both increase his debts. Jonathan and myself have been bailing him out for years and just when we think there's signs of improvement, he lapses again. It's a never-ending circle of self-destruction and now he's even got our own security team to aid his sickness."

"I'm sorry. I never knew."

Jerome presses on. "Please forward the written report as requested in our contract with your photos and final invoice. I'll gladly take care of it for you. Just two final things, Mr. Panther."

"Absolutely."

"Please, and I know I can rely on you, and I implore you, not a word to a soul. I'll deal with internal matters this end as I see fit."

Blackthorn feels truly sad for Jerome. "That goes without saying, and what's the second thing?"

"You'll be pleased to know I'm accepting your immediate resignation from the security department. Kindly return your uniform to the front desk when you drop in your report."

Blackthorn smiles. "Yes, I'll be sorry to leave you in the lurch, but I have other things to do. I'll be sure to drop off the report and uniform in the next day or so and look forward to the balance payment."

"Ah, yes. I hadn't forgot. Lewis said you would be worth every penny and he was right. Thanks again, Mr. Panther. It's Blackthorn, isn't it?"

"It is, yes."

Blackthorn enjoys a momentary feeling of importance. "Then, Mr. Blackthorn Panther, PI, it's been a pleasure doing business with you. Should you ever be in the need for fine feminine underwear, you know where to come."

"I'll bear it in mind, Mr. Jerome. Thanks."

The phone goes dead and Blackthorn decides that the day has started well enough. He needs now to phone Pete to get those photos developed so he can deliver the report, return the uniform and collect his check, as arranged. He's about to pick up again when an incoming call beats him to it.

"Hello, Panther Investigations. How may I help you?" He recognizes the female voice immediately and his heart misses a beat. "Hi Blacky Wolfman Panther, PI. I desperately need your help!"

About the Author

Jonty Olivier was born in Kidderminster, Worcestershire, England, and has spent most of his life storytelling and writing. Whether it be poetry, short stories, one-minute monologues, newspaper and radio commercials, he is known in close family and friends' circles as "The Word Wizard." Jonty is a former British police officer and private detective.